MW01480295

Fiction In Red

Airline Edition

Eddy Ivy

Eddy Ivy Press

Fiction in Red
Airline Edition
All Rights Reserved.
Copyright © 2009 Eddy Ivy
V3.0

Eddy Ivy Press

ISBN: 978-0-9822684-0-7

Library of Congress Control Number: 2008943788

PRINTED IN THE UNITED STATES OF AMERICA

Foreword

There are a collection of 27 off the wall short stories in this book. In order to enhance your reading experience a twist has been added. All of the words of this book which are in red lettering are fictional. These tales impart wisdom, promote intellect, evoke fantasies, enhance vocabulary, provide entertainment and install morals.

Special thanks to the following individuals.

Fiona McAuliffe, The cover artist who made my dream a reality.

Bonnie Darves, Oregon author, writer, for editing services and advice.

Table of Contents

1

A Friend In Need Is A Friend Indeed

L iving 10 miles out in the wooded countryside in the mid Oregon coast had its advantages and disadvantages when friends from town came to spend the weekend. Being out in the boonies with a lot of trees can be fun for about an hour or so, but not much more. Fortunately, we had many distractions from which to choose.

If we needed money, the golf course was full of ponds for hunting golf balls at night. We would go out in our one-man rubber rafts and feel around in the mud to retrieve one ball after another. A good night would net us 400 of the white spheres, which we would then sell to the clubhouse for 10 cents apiece. Twenty bucks a kid, in the 1970s, was a pretty good haul back then!

If we were into riding the trails we could go virtually anywhere in the hills behind my house. There were so many trails and interconnecting logging roads that virtually any type of small motorized vehicle was game. We had classic mini-bikes, mopeds, go-carts, dirt-bikes and even an electric bike in the mix of the dozen or so classmates that lived and played in those woods.

If it was too wet and rainy, we had a beach about 100 yards from my house. On many occasions we were instructed to go secure our dinner! Suiting up and grabbing a couple of shovels we would go out to the mud flats and dig for clams. It was a routine I knew well, and seldom did the whole affair last more than an hour. The butter clams, as we called them, made for a mean clam chowder.

One of my favorite adventures was catching trout in Gould's ponds. Rumor had it that Old Man Gould was a **shrewd** businessman. Whether this was true I did not know. What I did know was that he ran a rock quarry operation and that every hole he dug became **ecological** magic. You see, the five ponds of Gould's that I knew about all ranked among the best fishing holes I have ever fished in my life.

I could ride my bicycle six to eight miles and be at any one of his old quarries--and I'd catch my limit of rainbow trout any day of the week. What made his quarries special is that the nearby streams nearly always appeared to flow into one end and out the other--and all looked uncannily natural. Not surprisingly, the natural fish stocks flourished when they found these deep rock-based **havens**. The major benefit was that instead of living in a shallow streambed, the fish actually had a place to hide and rest on their way upstream.

The drawback of going "up the valley" was that it was, truly, all uphill. I had extra bikes and fishing poles and lures, not to mention a great story line. For some inexplicable (to me, anyway) reason, the prospect of riding a bike eight miles uphill didn't appeal to some of my city-slicker friends. To get them excited about making the trek I had invented this story: If you were man enough to walk through the Hanging Trees where **unsavory** and reputedly disgruntled ghosts still loomed, the spirit of Old Man Gould would enable you to catch a fish on your first cast out into any one of his manmade lakes.

The hanging trees were just a couple of 80-foot-tall Douglas firs that stood about five feet apart from each other. They were unique, however; at some point in time, an enterprising person had **grafted** the two together, by taking a branch from one and splicing it to the other resembling an H, so that the two trees appeared to be holding hands. At 30 some odd feet up, the cross member's girth was almost two feet through. Someone had spent a lot of time and energy creating that handhold. The **spectacle** was made all the more mysterious by the sign posted at the base of the trees that read: A friend in need is a friend indeed.

It was at this **juncture** in the woods one overcast weekend that I had hauled up my friend, Bob, to go fishing at the upper lake. Looking at the trees, then at me with a quizzical look, he said, "You don't really expect me to believe that hogwash about the first cast catch, do you?" Reluctant to admit that the "statistic" was my own invention or to disclose that Old Man Gould was still alive, I kept moving. I hopped the fence, sprinted over the crabgrass and through the trees, and hopped back on to my bike. Bob, still unimpressed, said, "I bet you five bucks that you don't catch a fish on your first cast! The moment of truth had arrived. I looked Bob squarely in the eye, and said, "You just lost five bucks, dude."

The first six miles on our bikes had been on pavement and the slight upgrade of a degree or two was gentle and easy, like the stream we were following. The final two miles were on a dirt and gravel logging road, which was fairly steep at times. Bob's confidence that he would win the bet made the two last steep and punishing miles uphill more bearable for him, but not for me. The incline really didn't bother me, but the $5 I was about to lose did, and Bob knew it.

On arriving at the old maintenance shack, we stopped for a moment. The ancient shed contained a **veritable quandary** of ancient **relics** would have normally been a delight for any 12-year-old boy. This shed was always open and looked like something from decades past. Old tools, and truck parts on shelves collecting dust, was the scene. Strangely, none of the relics appeared to be out of place, as if they were still waiting to be used by someone who would someday show up.

We didn't look for long because we had a bet, and I was

being pressured to cast the first cast. I looked in my tackle box and retrieved my favorite lure of all time, the one-ounce black and silver rooster tail. As much as I wanted to use it, I decided it wasn't my best shot because the day was overcast. So I nabbed another favorite, a large red oblong mirrored spoon that caught my eye. The reason to use this spoon was that it was flashier and a half-ounce heavier than the rooster tail. By attaching it I would also able to cast out about 20 feet farther.

Being careful not to tangle the treble hook on the end of the spoon I got a good footing. Aiming for one of the three small streams that fed this small man-made pond, I sent up a small prayer. The whip of my pole and the whirr of my line preceded the plop of my lure signaling a great cast of 60 feet. Giving a small pull to get the spoon to spin I got a bite within a few feet. The fight was on. It was no match, even though the eight-inch rainbow trout didn't have a chance and I was now a very happy boy.

Watching me pulse with pride, Bob became extraordinarily excited. He exclaimed, "Nobody catches a fish on the first cast. This place is awesome!" Pulling out a spoon of his own, he cast it out into the middle of the lake time after time and came up empty-handed. I, on the other hand, knew that the deep holes of the lake were just near where the streams and food entered the lake and kept on pulling out fish time after time Even though we were hitting close to the same spot he wasn't even getting a bite. Visibly upset, Bob snapped, "Hey, why are you catching fish and I'm not?"

I looked back, smugly, and said, "You didn't go through the hanging trees."

Moral of the story: If you're fishing for something, use the right bait!

2
A Toast

Have you ever had one of those bad hair days when your eyes are blurry, your mind is fuzzy, and everything seems to be moving in slow motion? Well, it was precisely one of those days, in the **doldrums** of December, when I stumbled out of bed and headed into the kitchen, without my prescription glasses.

Opening the mini-blind did not help my condition, since the sky was gray and it was raining drearily. Normally, I would make a full pot of coffee, but I was in no mood for any more work than was absolutely necessary. Bacon and eggs, ha! I thought not. A couple of slices of toast without butter would have to **suffice** this morning. A quick push down on the toaster's slide latch and a teaspoon of instant coffee for the instant hot water dispenser, and I was the king of the fastest breakfast a nearly blind zombie could feast upon.

It is amazing how fast a black cup of instant coffee made with a tablespoon of instant coffee will wake you up. In fact, there is only one thing on the face of this earth that will wake you up faster. Yes, you guessed it, a big mouthful of hot moldy toast.

You know the sensation I'm talking about, surely. You want to puke your guts out, and then you try to tell yourself that mold is good because it makes **penicillin**, and then you stretch over the sink hoping to aim for the center of the garbage disposal.

Looking back, I was actually glad that the coffee was instant; it would have been a shame to waste a real cup of Joe while trying to gargle and swish out the last **vestiges** of green crud from between my teeth. Not only was the newfound strength of my espresso-like brew enough to overpower the mold, it gave me **impetus** to try a couple of new pieces of bread to get rid of the taste of the overpowering **elixir**. Fortunately, I had a new loaf of wheat bread that I had purchased the day before at the supermarket.

Opening the breadbox and pulling out the loaf, I managed to tug at the end where the plastic quick-release guitar pick-style thingy is supposed to be, but instead found that the package was secured by one of those **confounding** paper-coated metal twisty ties that always, in my experience anyway, end up being twisted the wrong way.

After I endured the **agonizing** and surprisingly time-consuming process of trying to undo the darn thing, I finally got it open. I reached in to the plastic sack and tried to bypass the heel, but my fingers couldn't get ahold of anything. Frustrated, but knowing that I was **omnipotent** in comparison to that stupid loaf of bread, I wouldn't settle for defeat.

Well, in my mind I was of course saying, "I'll show this loaf of bread who's boss," and just as I grabbed a big handful of bread, to my surprise I realized that I'd yanked out the whole loaf! Grasping it with both hands and holding it up closer for further inspection a grin came to my face.

At that point I realized there are times in your life that you just have to laugh. That loaf of bread I'd wrestled with somehow had never made its way through the slicing machine! Then it dawned on me that just a few days earlier, I had found myself wishing for thicker slices of bread to fit in my oversized toaster slots. Still chuckling to myself I wondered what else my **importunate** approach might work on!

Moral of the story: Be careful about the things you wish for; they just might come true!

3

A View To Die For

Anyone who has ever worked in a U.S. National Park for a summer will readily report that there wasn't enough time to enjoy the park itself. There ought to be a law against requiring staff to work more than 30 hours a week in any of our treasured wilderness areas. Most people who sign on, do so for the opportunity to experience the wild beauty of our heritage that so many have worked tirelessly to preserve. Furthermore, anyone who doesn't live year round in the national park system should be exempt from federal income tax. I add this as a suggestion, as I also think that **concessionaires** would need to be compensated somehow so they can make a reasonable profit.

If this bill were to pass, those who work as public

servants in our national nature preserves might not be viewed merely as workers, but rather as individuals who go there because they want to appreciate and experience what the United States once was. There is no other place that I can think of where this privilege is remotely possible.

Quite by accident, one summer I found myself at Mount Rainier National Park in Washington, which was not my chosen workplace. The roof of the historic Crater Lake Lodge, in Oregon, where I had worked before and planned to spend the summer, had caved in from the weight of the snow. This failure forced the closure of the main restaurant for the season. Arriving home so to speak with no place to sleep, let alone work, was cause for quite a commotion among those of us who had arrived ready to work at Crater Lake.

Fortunately, my previous season's manager, Bob, was a caring man who was on top of the situation. He had found job offers for his entire crew of displaced workers—even before we had learned that we didn't have jobs. The positions were in parks throughout the western United States, with a wide range of concessionaires.

That turn of events took me all the way up to a waiter's position in Paradise Lodge at Mount Rainier. When I got up there, the lodge management was desperate for more workers, so I suggested one of my outdoorsy hunting buddies, Tom, who had just graduated from Lewis and Clark College in Portland, Oregon. With no other immediate plans, he agreed and made the four-hour trip the next day. Blessed with one of those semi-photographic memories Tom was hired on the spot when the manager handed him a menu and he read back the specials and prices after only a short glance.

Deciding where to go on a day off can be a challenge if you can't agree with your hiking buddy beforehand. To deal with that dilemma, my roommate, Tom, had come up with an interesting tie-breaking system for those times we couldn't come to a **melding** of our mindsets. We would take a **topographical** map and pin it to our dartboard and then proceed to each throw a dart from across the room. We would then take a **straight-edge** and make our destination the nearest water feature, located somewhere along the line between the darts, unless of course we both had been there before.

In this fashion, we wound up in some interesting places. One lake we visited was near a point of interest called Pinnacle Peak. Daring the 45-percent grade with telescoping fishing poles in our backpacks, we found that the lake we had worked so hard to get to was **sterile**. That is to say, the water was so cold since it was only fed through snow pack that it couldn't sustain life like a lake fed by small streams providing nutrients does.

Another dart-fully planned outing late in the season found us at a trailhead on the southern side of the mountain. It was a trail that ran parallel to the road but was located on the other side of a huge canyon. We had passed it many times but had never bothered to research it. As we were **sticklers** about carrying out our dart-pinned adventures, we decided to carry out our plan. We chose to trek the eastern side of the all uphill 12-mile trail and leave the four-mile leg for another outing. Our pinpointed destination was also the largest lake on the loop. This lake, which we nicknamed Thimbleberry, looked promising in the view category, from what we could surmise by looking at it on our topographical map.

Normally, we left the details of our hike plans with neighboring bunkmates. But that morning, we were getting off to a late start and couldn't find anyone around. Heeding the pre-season park rangers' advice, we did the next best thing—we left a document, which indicated our start time, direction, destination, and expected return time, folded on the dash of the car before we took off.

Approximately 193 minutes later, we arrived at our destination. The layout of the lake was **symmetrically** egg shaped, with the narrowed end facing south. The far end, roughly 200 yards away, offered what looked like a sandy beach and an opening in the trees. We hypothesized that it might be a waterfalls headwater, hence delivering on the promise of the **grandiose** view we had been expecting.

Unfortunately for us, the entire lengths of the lake's sides were lined with insurmountable Himalaya blackberry bushes. As hard as we tried, we could not find a trail or any way over to get to the other side of the lake--which we had previously deemed to have a cliff-like ledge running **perpendicular** to it as indicated by the contour lines of our map of the area. As we had been planning to end up at this lake in any event, we decided to swim our way across and to further explore the beach area across the lake.

Stepping in tentatively, we turned to each other and smiled, remarking on how warm the lake was compared to others we had been in earlier in the season. We chalked it up to the sunny day and early August being the warmest month of the year. About two thirds of the way across we agreed to stop. The water was freezing, and we were both starting to feel it. We had both noted how cold the water had become, and how quickly the temperature had changed, but until then we hadn't felt the need to stop. Now both of us were starting to cramp up, and we had to make a critical decision. Self-preservation took over, and we headed for the nearest bank which was, ironically, our original destination.

Arriving at the bank we found that our beach was, in fact, a raft of logs. Climbing onto the bank, we were relieved and headed over to the ledge to find a grand view from the edge of a cliff. Gaining this vantage point's remote and **surreptitious** location was the very reason we were working in the park. After we had warmed up in the mid-day sun, we realized that we had a huge problem. Analyzing our situation from the embankment, we saw that the water on this end of the lake was a deep green-black, and therefore, likely to be 40 to 50 feet deep. Our entry into the other end had been warm because the sun's rays were penetrating the lake's **shoal** bottom, and that in turn heated the shallow waters.

Exacerbating the situation were the thorns of hell lining the ledges of the lake all the way into the water's depths. Convinced that we might not make it back alive if we swam across, we came up with an idea: We would find a log that would support us, and swim back alongside it, in case we cramped up again.

We not only cramped up. It happened a whole lot quicker this second time around, and it was far more severe. Even the ripples in our muscles that weren't cramping up were in themselves painful. Fortunately, the effects of our painful **pre-hypothermia** began to subside when we got back to the southern side of the lake.

About 20 feet from the shore, we were startled to see a man standing on the shore watching us. All day we hadn't seen a soul, and now, in the middle of nowhere, from out of nowhere, here was a guy asking us how the water was. "Freezing," I blurted, through chattering teeth. Not skipping a beat, my buddy, Tom said, "You might want to take your wife and children down to the next lake, which has a picnic table." Looking up, I saw his family in the distance who were obviously trying to catch up with their **callous** father at about 50 yards up the trail.

"Well, this is a national park," he said **curtly**, "and I am going to have lunch and enjoy the view from here." Sensing an argument and a serious fight in the making, I replied, in defense of my friend, "If you don't leave in 30 seconds, you, and your family are going to have two magnificent views." This, as I pointed to some nearby shrubs containing all of our clothes.

Moral of the story: Don't be a dip in the woods.

4
Angel Hair Chimney

Debbie was a Fourth of July baby. She would constantly remind me of this **trite** piece of information throughout the months of May and June. It occurred to me that Debbie's **incessant** reminder of this patriotic holiday had nothing whatsoever to do with independence, but rather was her way of ensuring presents from me on that special day.

One of the more memorable presents I gave Debbie to mark her never ending birthday was a camping trip to Timothy Lake near Mount Hood in Oregon. Now, it's important to know that Debbie's idea of camping was to book an expensive hotel **situated** in a woodsy spot. In fact, if we were out on any of our excursions and she saw a resort or classy Bed & Breakfast, she would just whip out her credit card and use it as a pointer. It wasn't that she didn't like the great outdoors, it was just that sleeping bags don't come in satin.

Debbie's **predilection** for structure in nature meant we normally visited a lot of beautifully maintained gardens. This usually meant that the free recreational areas I preferred were **verily** missed. Once, while we were pulling into the parking lot of the Trees of Mystery in northern California, the following conversation ensued:

"Geez, Debbie, why are we going to pay to see a bunch of funny-looking deformed trees? We could have stopped just outside of Crescent City and walked down that scenic trail and seen a forest full of grand-looking redwoods for free."

"Eddy, think about it. That trail sign said 'The **Damnation** Trail.' Just what part of damnation don't you understand?"

Yes, Debbie could be fairly described as a fair-weather camper, and our birthday adventure at Timothy Lake that year was to be no exception. In order to transport all of our extra "necessities" across the lake, we had to attach my hand-crafted version of an **outrigger** to the canoe. This invention, originally intended to provide a safe platform that enabled me to stand upright to fish--normally a big no-no in any small craft—gave us the space and means to carry two huge Army surplus radio boxes, which we filled with our **"indispensable rations."**

Eddy Ivy

It was a relief, to say the least, when we arrived, heavily laden with gear, at the far shore of the lake. We had been caught in one of those freak thunderstorms to which Oregon is no stranger. The dark storm clouds and the lightning strikes were bearable enough, and probably would have been exhilarating, had we already made camp. The problem was that it was freezing cold in the middle of summer and we were in tank top T-shirts. The hail and rain hitting the water meant that not only were we getting wet from the sky above, but the splashing from the frozen **precipitate** on the lake was also **dousing** us from all sides. We both resembled half-drowned rats, **albeit** shivering ones, on account of our half-hour ordeal.

Normally, I would have forgone building a campfire at noon in July. But as we had two gallons of Coleman fuel for our two lanterns and camp stove, about 10 times what we probably needed for three days, and since I was determined to make my birthday girl happy at any cost at this point, I decided to splurge. Fortunately we had brought along a good three day's supply of dry firewood, lighting this fire was going to be a snap. The anticipation of a hot crackling campfire was very comforting indeed.

Unscrewing the cap of the fuel container, I looked at Debbie authoritatively and said, "Promise me you won't do this." She seemed **coherent** and attentive enough when she muttered, "OK, Eddy." But I knew Debbie. So to further my **resolve** to communicate the message that what I was about to do was *not* something to be attempted by an inexperienced person, I said, "I've been doing this for years and have had a couple of close calls myself." I

18

further explained that my method was the only sure way to burn off the old insulation from used copper wire, which I used to sell for scrap at metal recycling centers.

"So, Debbie, do you really understand that this is dangerous and that people are sometimes hospitalized because they do something like this when they don't know what they are doing?" Looking a bit annoyed at that point, Debbie nodded again. I was sure she understood this time.

I found eight half-burnt logs near the fire pit and arranged them in the English style, resembling a two-storied tick-tack-toe structure. Then I layered up more of our new dry fireplace logs in a similar fashion. I took out my stainless steel Sierra Club hiker's cup and measured out two cups of white gas directly onto the charred wood. An additional cup was lightly sprinkled over the newer logs. Then I sprinkled two more cups into the coals, which readily soaked up the moist fuel.

In final preparation, I took my forefinger and started a shallow **furrow** in the damp dirt just outside the fire ring. When finished it was eight feet in length leading straight out to the lowest point of the campfire area. This was important because our fire ring was slightly elevated, and gas fumes **migrate** downward and tend to pool in low areas creating a severe fire hazard.

Then it was time for the show. I poured a thin stream of gas in the trough to fashion a "**fuse**" of sorts. Walking toward my trench fuse with a match at ground level, the fumes ignited about a foot away from the end of my finger furrowed ditch. Presto! The fireball followed the half inch channel for eight feet and ignited the firewood in an instant, and we were cooking hotdogs and drying off in no time.

The next morning I woke up to Debbie's blood-curdling scream. She had taken it upon herself to pour out about a half gallon of gas on some of our unused wood, and then walked back to draw a channel in the dirt to make a fuse, as she'd watched me do the afternoon before. Unfortunately for our **heroine**, the attempt went poorly. The coals from the night before had **spontaneously** ignited the gas fumes, just as Debbie was bending down to stick her finger in the now dry ground.

Her bangs caught fire and her eyebrows were singed. By the time I was out of the tent she had put out the fire by rolling herself in the dew-**laden** grass nearby. She was in too much shock to cry. I wrapped my arms around her and, in between planting a couple of nice wet ones on her now moist lips. I laughed and said, "This proves that hot chicks are nothing but trouble in the woods, doesn't it?"

Finally, she started to laugh, too, and we went back to the fire to face her latest fear. Fortunately the only injury she sustained was the **frayed** burnt ends of her hair. Incredibly, she had incurred no burn marks or scorching to her face. Thinking quickly, I tended to her bangs as best I could with my multitool's scissors attachment. Then I silently thanked God for Leatherman tools and decided I had better make her as comfortable as possible.

Bringing out a blanket and a pillow, I gently instructed Debbie to sit down and take it easy in one of our comfy chairs, and said, "I'll make you your favorite drink--and then I'll start breakfast." Preparing her cherished beverage, an Indian Coolie Loachie, I boiled milk, added in a heaping teaspoon of instant coffee, and then **doctored** it up with a generous shot of Amaretto. (This little trick makes the occasional pine needle in the scrambled eggs a lot more bearable for everyone involved.)

After breakfast we found ourselves lying back facing each another in the fancy lounge chairs we'd brought along--way too expensive, at eighty bucks apiece, but worth every penny.

Now calm, Debbie piped up, out of the blue, "Eddy, I've seen a lot of people go by on the trail this morning, but no one has waved back at me or even bothered to look our way. Don't you think that's a little odd?"

"Maybe the smell of burnt hair is a people-**repellent**," I said, half laughing. Giving me the evil eye and a crooked smile, she retorted, "Noooo! I'm serious, Eddy. Why don't you go over to the trail and see why people aren't waving back at us?"

I groaned while turning my lounge chair toward the forest trail to witness what I figured was just a figment of her imagination. It didn't take long before a couple of hikers came ambling by, just 25 yards from our campsite. Waving at people in such close proximity and receiving no response, the realization hit home that Debbie wasn't imagining the fact that we were being ignored. And I simply couldn't believe that no one was waving back or stopping by to visit, as most Oregonians do when they come upon friendly fellow campers.

Adding up the facts I ascertained that the setting we were in was fairly common and resembled most of Oregon's natural forests. We were surrounded by tall timber, which was fairly well thinned out and open to help prevent forest fires. There were numerous clumps of wild sword ferns in all directions, and we were positioned between the lake and the trail. Something just didn't add up in my mind, and I was determined to figure out our vexing social situation.

Anyone who enjoys a challenge or a mystery will appreciate my **paranoia** about this bizarre, unusual series of events. Our seeming invisibility was beginning to really **gnaw** on me. After all, we had loads of gear all around us, a tent that stood out like a sore thumb, and a small but visually **serenading** campfire, to boot. Pretty hard to miss, I reasoned.

First standing up, then sitting down to take another hit off of my **decadently** flavored "morning cap," my curiosity finally got the better of me. I started proceeding up a **spur** trail to the main trail. Within seconds, Debbie's mystery had been solved, but it took a few minutes for me to become convinced of what my eyes appeared to be showing me. Shaking my head in disbelief, I walked back through the low brush and sword ferns and couldn't see anything but "woods", until I was a mere 20 feet from our site. I plunked myself down on the lounge chair and started laughing heartily.

"Well, what is so funny?" Debbie asked.

"You're not going to believe this, but you actually can't *see* this campsite from the trail," I explained. "The ferns and small brush hide all of our gear and the blue tent is almost the exact same color as the lake behind us, which effectively **camouflages** us from the trail. In fact, the only way I was able to see this site was from the swirling **translucent** angel hair waves of heat rising up from our campfire."

She looked at me and said, "You're right, Eddy, I don't believe you!" Standing up with her Coolie Loachie she proceeded over to the trail. Watching her curving moves as she wound her way through the brushy ferns I smiled as I admired her feminine beauty. Turning about face 180 degrees she moved her head to the left and then to the right, almost in panic she cried out, "I don't believe this, where are you?"

I laughed heartily and yelled back, "Right here, Debbie, underneath the angel hair chimney!"

Moral of the story: Other people rarely see the same view you do; to see the whole picture, sometimes you need to physically put yourself in the other person's place.

5

Avalanche!

From the time I was nine years old I had always been around guns. This was in spite of the fact that my dad had **dyslexic** eyesight and wasn't exactly what you would call a hunting **enthusiast**. During his two-year stint as a police officer on the Fort Peck Indian Reservation he would tell woeful stories to remind me and my pre-teen friends that firearms were not toys.

He taught me how to shoot, care for and respect all of the guns in our house. Under his supervision I was shown how to break down and clean his police revolver, army-issued rifle, and even his antique flint-locks. The most important rule was one that he reminded me of often, and that he thought should be taught to all children at an early age. It is simply this: If you come across a gun, don't touch it, and tell an adult immediately.

One of my favorite **pastime**s upon receiving my first .22 rifle at 16 years of age has been target shooting. Even though I prefer bow hunting to this day for big game, I still find that there is just something satisfying about going out into the woods and shooting up targets to your hearts content.

On one such outing, a hunting buddy, Tom, and I had just got finished shooting about a thousand rounds of ammo each, out of nearly a dozen different guns. The morning **extravaganza** left our steel targets none the worse for wear, as they were **specifically** designed for this purpose. (We had decided years earlier that blowing up fruit, glass jars and mowing down small trees with bullets just wasn't as much fun somehow, as it had been in our teens.)

A little before noon, we took a break and decided to check out a wide trail on the high side of our practice range. During past outings, we had always wondered where that trail led, but we had never taken the time to properly check it out. This was the day. We locked the truck, grabbed some lunch, and took off.

About 300 yards into our trek we discovered that the trail had once been a logging road. This passage had been washed out, quite literally, due to a huge rock slide. Everything within its path including trees, brush, dirt and even life itself had been washed away down the hill. In fact, everything within a half mile on the hillside was gone. Up the hill, down the hill, across the face, the scene was a river of irregularly shaped gray rocks. These chunky, **lichen**-laden boulders were from 12 inches to 60 inches in diameter, seemingly frozen in place, waiting for the perfect time to thaw.

Judging from the dormant gray moss clinging beneath many of the stout **spheres**, we deemed the slide stable and proceeded to traverse the gray landscape. About half way across the rock field we came upon a large boulder. This **totem** stood out amongst the rugged carpet of small boulders, its size alone gave it the appearance of instability. Surveying the steep **terrain**, we saw a slow-moving stream, about 20 feet wide, dissecting the bottom of the steep valley.

We looked at each other in mild amusement, and for a moment, read each other's minds. What might happen, we thought, if we set this newfound play toy in motion down to the stream below?

Initially, we tried to push it over by hand, but we quickly discovered that it was **anchored** much more solidly that it first appeared to be. Moving this **monolith** would call for "the big guns," we soon realized. Using a couple of nearby branches of **dubious** value and unknown substance we prodded the rock, to no avail. Indeed the branches broke due to dry rot and we almost **conceded** defeat.

We took a break, ate lunch, and came up with Plan B:

We needed to find bigger levers, so we decided to use **fulcrums** in our next attempt. That combination of stronger and longer poles worked. Fashioning an **impromptu** teeter-totter, we pumped up and down over and over until we rocked our steadfast opponent over the brink. Thus, our plan of using leverage made the job a **cinch**.

As soon as we sent the rock on its way down, we moved to the side of the rock slide that we were, a moment earlier, **bisecting**. We had seen avalanches before and knew that we didn't want to be caught in the middle of one if the whole side of the hill gave way. This slide was stable, as we had determined, so nothing rumbled or gave way.

What struck us was the snail's pace at which the boulder sauntered down the hill. On several occasions, it appeared to stop and then wobble backwards as if to purposefully deceive us into believing it had stopped for good, before resuming its travels. After what seemed an **eternity**, the rock did begin to pick up a little speed, but what happened next was disappointing.

Next to the streambed was a huge **deciduous** broadleaf tree. It was the only tree for a quarter mile in either direction, and our boulder hit it dead center. We looked at each other and laughed; only we could be unlucky enough to miss the stream! I joked that that we wouldn't have been able to hit that tree in a million years if we have been trying, yet our Big Splash had been **thwarted** at the last second by an obstacle neither one of us had foreseen.

As upsetting as our failed attempt to speed up the

gravity of nature was, we proceeded back across the slide to continue our hike anyway. In our haste, we did not realize that something far more spectacular than our original plan was about to happen.

We didn't get our huge splash, and no, the tree didn't fall over. But the rock's collision with the tree had loosened all of its pollen, which, as there wasn't a breath of wind, hovered suspended in the air and began drifting slowly up the valley.

The sight was breath-taking. The pollen formed a **vibrant** yellow ball measuring approximately 60 feet in diameter—the "cloud" was so dense that we couldn't see through it. The late afternoon sunshine enveloped the pollen mass, giving it an **eerie**, **iridescent** glow and making it appear remarkably like a hot air balloon without a basket..

Dumbstruck, we simply sat down and watched. The spellbinding show went on for 10 minutes before our view was obstructed. Our pollen cloud floated behind a stand of tall Douglas firs, but the reflection of the sunshine hitting the yellow mass though the trees seemed to sparkle good-bye, good-bye! I'll always be grateful, somehow, that our boulder missed its mark.

Moral of the story: Most advances in human history come from observing and analyzing mistakes and anomalies. So can enjoyment.

6

Bear Cave

My high school buddy, Marvin, had worked for so long at Crater Lake that he had the privilege of having his own room in the main lodge with a stunning view of the lake. While visiting him one morning, about two weeks into my first employment there as a VIP dishwasher, Marvin said, "Eddy, look at the lake."

Turning around quickly, I expected to see something profound in the hypnotic deep blue jewel. Turning back to Marvin, after breaking the lake's spell, I said, dismissively, "Yes, Marvin, it's still there. It looks like no one has pulled the plug yet."

Laughing out loud and then walking over to the picture

window Marvin retorted, "I've been here a few years, Eddy, and I've never seen the lake so perfectly calm before."

Looking out his window, I discovered, eerily, that he was correct. There wasn't a single wave, ripple or wind sweep anywhere across the lake's surface. It was so clear that you could see the reflection of Phantom Ship, Wizard Island and a couple of small clouds slowly making their way across the mirrored **plane**.

Speaking up again, Marvin informed me that the Klamath Indians held a belief, long ago, that if a person were to make a wish while the lake was at peace, that wish would eventually come true. "OK. I want a raise!" I pronounced jokingly. "Eddy, Bob already gave you one," he told me.

Darn it! What a waste of a wish, I thought. Or was Marvin just trying to get me back for the **hanging-trees** prank I had pulled on him and so many of my other friends? That morning had been almost four years earlier, and now I was once again at Crater Lake. But this time it was in mid-winter. It was my school's winter break, and I had finished my master's **thesis** research and the final tests, in my not-so-humble opinion. Getting away from it all was all I could think of to try to clear my head.

I guess I was bracing myself for the storm that was to follow during my spring term. For the heck of it, I had requested my master's diploma a year early. I had found a loophole in the graduate program requirements and was able to take extra classes most people chose to ignore. Somehow I knew that the stark and chilly **despondency** of the icy lake would calm the anxiety of that future event, by focusing my thoughts well beyond what lay ahead.

Outside the main entrance at the gift shop and grill at Rim Village I peered in. Happily, I found that I recognized all of the faces there. The devoted skeleton crew of six were all good friends from years gone by! Nervously, I walked in, wondering if they had seen me **perusing** the lake and what their reaction to my arrival would be.

Happily, I was greeted by a unison cry from all six. "Hi, Eddy! Want a job?" Guess I'm kind sort of unforgettable, I thought to myself, grinning.

It turned out that the place was short handed and the crew needed help with the annual gift shop inventory for a few days. As I was already planning on working there for the summer in the restaurant and it was a given that a few extra bucks wouldn't hurt, I readily took the offer.

After my first **harrowing** day of assuming my **tedious** counting duties in the shop I was ready to crash for the night. Just then, Dale, the head cook and a co-worker from four years earlier, said, "Hey, Eddy. What do you want-- prime rib or rib eye?"

"You sure know how to keep people here, don't you, Dale!" I responded gleefully. "In that case, I'll take the rib eye." Dale reminded me that few people, even the Crater Lake devotees like him, were insane enough to stick around for the winter. "So you might as well take advantage of everything remaining from the main lodge leftovers," he said.

After consuming a very satisfying dinner, I posed the inevitable question: What else do you do around here in the middle of winter? Pointing at his mountain bike, Dale said, "Obstacle course! If you're not into slow tight maneuvers, side hops, four-inch balance-beam riding, hopping up and over make-believe logs, and then timing yourself in and around two restaurants with a stair climb and then the descent, you don't know what **desolation** is all about!

For five days, that was the only fun we had to look forward to in the evening. Fortunately, all good things must come to an end. I somewhat regretfully said good-bye to Dale, Marvin and the other die-hards. This **adieu** occurred only after I had confirmed my work date well before anyone else had the chance to pick the prime summer-season spots!

Returning to the lake was to happen sooner than I had planned, however. It turned out that all of the extra classes I had taken during the year and the summer had indeed been added into my required core **curriculum**, at my request. Almost by mistake, I had finished my Master's in Business Administration program in one year instead of two!

The **maelstrom** of debates that followed behind closed doors, as I was told by several professors, was squarely centered on me. This **charade**, to the **chagrin** of a few of the professors, and the amusement of others, was **quelled** by the president of the college. When he asked the **furtive** assembly which classes I would have to take to meet the minimum requirements, no one responded in any detail. They all realized, seemingly in unison, that I had ingeniously managed to take all of the required classes needed to earn my degree in one year by loading up on summer-session classes.

Not having to pay for another year of college and having my graduate degree in hand was exhilarating. Finding a desk job, on the other hand, wasn't an exciting prospect--or even on my mind, for that matter. Calling up the concessions manager at the lodge, I was told that they could use my services as soon as I could get up to the lake. I wouldn't have to wait for the main lodge to open to begin opening bottles as a wine steward.

After enduring more snow in a couple of months than most people will enjoy in a lifetime, the sun began making an appearance. The huge snow drifts began melting, and even the snow cave that Dale and Marvin had dug, was slowly giving way to March's brightening spring weather.

One morning, we were doing spring cleaning and stocking Oregon's largest gift shop, which was sited, according to legend, precisely where two dainty bulls had once frolicked, when we heard a huge crash. Going to the window and looking outside, we saw a small (roughly 250-pound) brown bear rooting through the garbage cans--and having a grand time of it. We weren't going out, and he wasn't going anywhere. We watched him for about 20 minutes while he ate anything that he could maneuver into the confines of his mouth.

It wasn't long before a car drove up and scared him off, but for the next two days we all had to use our cars for the short half-mile trip from our quarters to the gift shop and restaurant, to ensure our safety because the bear's paw prints went right past the back of our **barracks**. Finally, the rangers were able to capture him in one of those creative contraptions made out of a road culvert. They carted him away to happier (for him, we hoped, but certainly for us!) pastures down the mountain.

Since it was now relatively safe to go out now, I was determined to find out where this bear had spent most of his winter before he decided to come out of his **hibernation** early. Having access to a good pair of snow shoes, I started my search from the main lodge. It turned out that the bear had indeed been within 20 feet of the back of our barracks, but obviously had been uninterested in our empty trashcan as evidenced by the **beeline** he had made toward the odor of what to him had been a feast.

The bear's prints were coming straight from the lake, and the tracking was surprisingly easy to decipher, even in the waning light of that overcast afternoon. Reaching the rim of the caldera, I witnessed a sight that I hadn't seen in a long time: The lake was completely calm. And before even thinking about it, I wished that I would find that bear's den. Oops! I self-corrected and thought to myself, maybe there are still more bears in that den!

Looking down, it was evident that the bear had come up the incline of the slope from the lake. When I looked to the right of where I was then standing, it appeared that a mini-avalanche had taken place in the previous few days. Mr. Bear had come from somewhere across the way and, it now seemed, had been caught in the freefall. I could just imagine what it had been like, a cold breeze chilling his nose, the feeling of weightlessness, the small pine trees coming closer and closer.

"Hey, I'm not imagining this at all!" I assured my by-now somewhat shaken self. Falling on my rear, I tried to keep my clumsy, well-attached snowshoes in front of me while I dug into the snow with my hands. My freefall was short lived; stopping after about 100 yards, I was exceedingly grateful that I would not be taking an unplanned swim. I took off one snowshoe and reasoned that I could use it as a **deadman**.

By placing it vertically in the snow as an anchor, I reasoned that I would have something to pull against. Using the leg it had come out of, I would push my foot about two feet down into the snow as a second anchor. Even with my **improvised** technique, it took me nearly an hour to get back to the top of the rim.

When I got back to the **bunkhouse** I pulled out my map and made some notes on an expensive topographical map I had received as a gift selection after my **stint** helping with inventory just months earlier. The map **depicted** trails and features that most of the newer maps didn't have, and I used some fancy calculations and penciled in lines to mark the places I would try to go later in the summer, as my hope of finding the bear's retreat was now out of the question.

Two months later my quest rekindled when I unraveled my maps one day. Oh, yes. Inspecting my handiwork, I saw that the bear's **lair** was right in front of me. The best place for a bear to hibernate would be in one of two areas: the high ridges near the edge of the lake or a shelf-like canyon running parallel to the barracks.

I spent three weekends going back and forth in a grid-like pattern, over and over. I came up empty-handed every time. Finally, giving up and surmising that since the bear had been so small he likely didn't have an established den, I decided that he thus had no choice but to come out of hibernation early.

Of course, I had made my wish while looking deeply into that flat evil-looking glass, and fate awaited. Hiking across a meadow one day to take a picture of the lake, I was overcome by an unusual but overwhelming urge to stop. There was an oddity to the place, as if something was steering me to a hill in the opposite direction of where I was headed. Coming to a grassy knoll and looking up at a 45-degree-angled slope, the sight of a small hole in the side of a small outcropping of rock was barely visible to my naked eye.

Pulling out my binoculars, I saw that the hole was roughly the size of a rocking chair. Up I went, being drawn; it seemed, by an irresistible force—a feeling that, to my mind, doesn't happen too many times in one's life.

Could this be my bear's cave? It was a lot further up than I thought and the opening kept getting bigger and bigger. Reaching the entrance in a cold sweat, I realized that the opening was huge in comparison to my original estimate. It was at least nine feet high, and it went into solid rock for about 20 feet. Cautiously entering the opening, I discovered, fortunately, that there were no inhabitants. On the right-hand side there was a massive 90-square-foot shelf, where an entire family of bears could den for the winter in complete comfort. Looking around, I searched for more evidence. Was that bear fur or Bigfoot hair? The test results still haven't come in.

Moral of the story: I obviously should have wished for $1 million each time. But as I didn't, I will sell to anyone the location coordinates to my bear cave for $10,000 cash. Thank you.

7

Boulder Dash

Being granted an extra week to burn before my first summer in Ashland, Oregon, was a welcome gift from my understanding boss at Pizza Shack. I had wanted to hike the entire length of the Oregon section of the Pacific Crest Trail before leaving reality and joining the workforce, that early June in 1986. With my pack in tow I fashioned a bold cardboard sign that boldly proclaimed: PCT Trailhead, Happy Camp, California. It wasn't long before an amused traveler offered me a ride in the back of a small Subaru Brat pickup.

I had already scoped out the exact location of the trailhead while I was on a day trip on my lightning-fast Kawasaki KZ 650. Even though there was a pullout for the trailhead, **grizzled** experience had taught me that they are easy to miss. About two hours later I tapped on the back window and was dropped off just outside Seiad Valley, where the Pacific Crest Trail intersects Highway 96. After I thanked my **host chauffeur** profusely, he just shook his head and said, "Good luck, kid." Heading up the trail, it dawned on me that almost an entire day had been lost in transit. Now I just wanted to make up some lost time.

My 60-mile **ramble** with my heavy backpack would take me all the way up to nearly the summit of Mount Ashland and then drop me back down to Pilot Rock, near Interstate 5. There, figured, I would easily hitch a ride back to Ashland.

I had planned on a **vigorous** first two days to see how far I could get, and then two days of relaxing and catching up on reading and just taking it easy. So far, the only thing I had been able to accomplish was relaxing by the side of the road with a now dog-eared sign and a few spurts of reading a pocketbook in the back of a bumpy old pickup truck, that smelled mightily, I might add, of an ancient basset hound. Oh well, I thought, beggars can't be choosers.

Fortunately for me, at that juncture, my decision to pack lightly had paid off. Despite having stashed five days worth of rations in case of an emergency, my backpack was nonetheless roughly 16 pounds lighter than the 45 pounds it ordinarily weighed. As I was in a hurry, or so I had decided, I pushed onward until it became difficult to **visually** locate the white-**crested** markers high up in the trees.

Locating a flat spot 10 feet off the trail I set up camp in record time and dozed off quickly and soundly, arising six hours later, at dawn chomping to get back on the trail—and fiercely determined to make up more lost time. Since the cool morning air was invigorating I made good progress. By noon I had figured out that I was actually a couple of miles ahead of my planned trip and would be able to take it easy from there on out.

Under normal circumstances, in a setting like the infrequently traveled depths of the Pacific Crest Trail, one meets up with a minimum of one person per day on average. These encounters tend to cluster around trailheads and sections that are easily accessed by the notorious "**wannabe** hikers" (that's what we who are serious call them, anyway). These enthusiasts are easily distinguished by their fanny packs and the **obligatory** dual water bottles, stashed neatly in the sleek "stay-cold" pockets on the sides.

Oddly, I hadn't seen anyone for over a day and a half. The lack of people, logging roads--and wildlife for that matter--was a little strange with respect to most of my hikes. This welcome **quietude**, coupled with a disappointing lack of interesting **geological** formations, drove me on doggedly toward the day's end despite my resolution to relax.

The second night was much like the first. I prepared and consumed a fast meal, quickly pitched my tent, and dropped my sleeping bag on to an unusually and blessedly soft patch of ground. At dusk, I peered across my campsite and spied what appeared to be a picnic table in the middle of nowhere. On further inspection, I recognized the incredibly well-maintained setup as a horse rider's camp that my map, had I chosen to consult it, would have pointed out. Despite my dismay at the "invasion" of my space, I decided to call it a day anyway. After all, I had closed in on Mount Ashland at last, and that, surely, made for a commendable effort.

After waking up late from my well-deserved slumber, I decided that a good cup of "real coffee" was in order. For the record, if you want a real jolt some cold, damp morning on the trail, opt for the hiker's favorite: sheepherder's coffee, which is concocted by stirring in a couple teaspoons of Columbia's finest into a cup of boiling water and pretending that the grounds are **roughage**.

Since the sturdy table was available and potable water was nearby, I was quickly tantalized by the thought of a hearty, large breakfast. Why not? I thought, already virtually enjoying a can of bacon and AlpineAire no-cook mountain-style chili, topped with dried French-fried onions and doused liberally with a mini bottle of Tabasco sauce. Wow, my belly reminded me. That's a taste combination will stay with you forever—of just about--if you know what I mean.

After grudgingly washing more dishes than I had been required to reckon with in the previous three days in the nearby stream, I found that he task of breaking camp a relative breeze. Satisfied that I had everything in its rightful place, and that the only leftovers were ant-sized portions, then slowly I began my climb up the back side of Mount Ashland.

When I arrived near the ski lodge parking lot at about noon, I placed my pack on the trail and took a look around. Yep, it was still the same old lodge as it was in winter, where I had skied so many times before, just missing its lovely shawl of snow. Going back to my pack, I spied a large rock, and I decided that it looked to be a good spot for reading the class schedule for the upcoming year. After pulling out two cans of smoked oysters, a plastic toothpick, and the fall schedule, I decided to leave the pack where it was on the trail--an easy choice given that I had been moving uphill all morning.

Sitting on the edge of the seven-foot-high boulder with my feet dangling off the edge, I popped off the pull top of the can of oysters. Heaven was mine at that moment; a cool refreshing breeze swept up from below and the hot afternoon sun was being reflected off the tops of the fir trees. I literally had it made in the shade and my favorite seafood was in no short supply.

Within minutes I had started in on my second can of oysters, when an item on the class schedule caught my interest. Scuba diving! Wow, that looks like fun, I thought, and furthermore, the long-**intriguing** learning experience would even be covered by my tuition!

Smiling to myself as if I'd unexpectedly encountered a dime on the sidewalk, my attention was pulled away by the sight of a cute little brown bear snacking on a huckleberry bush about 100 yards below me. Looking back down at my schedule, I shifted gears when the realization--"Hey, that's a bear, you idiot!"--hit home.

A second look confirmed that the furry beast was no illusion or hallucination. Mentally countering my bewilderment, I jumped off my boulder and ran **laterally** 60 yards toward my pack at full speed. Grabbing my knife and whistle, I turned around and found no bear below. Spinning around I saw him 25 yards above the boulder at the parking lot intently looking at me. The small bear had just covered more than twice the distance uphill that a college runner, in top shape, had just run on a flat surface.

Watching him for a minute, with my **Bowie** knife in hand and my whistle in my mouth, I was now safe. Not because of the knife but because of the whistle, actually, and the fact that the bear was up above me and I therefore had the advantage. Why, one might well ask? It's because bears have short front legs and can run uphill fast, but they can't run downhill very well at all. Despite the fact that I had six miles of all downhill terrain before me, I could easily have made it to the highway before the bear did, if need be.

Besides that, I knew from my extensive reading that bears can't stand loud noises like rocks being smacked together, and the blast of air I pushed into that whistle was as long and as hard as my lungs could hold out. With the noise, the bear instantly dropped off its haunches, spun around, and ran off. Cute little fellow I thought to myself, heart pounding like a jack hammer!

Determined to finish my oysters and find my class schedule, which I had dropped in haste, this time when I sat down, the backpack stayed with me.

Moral of the story: Know your adversary.

8

Boxcar

The Oregon coast sand dunes are a fantastic place to play if you have the right toys. There was one particular place, which we called Boxcar, where my good buddy and high school classmate, John, especially liked to go. The spot was appropriately named, as there was a rail line situated alongside a massive sand dune, which made for easy loading whenever someone needed a train full of sand.

To make the trip a little more interesting, we usually would make it a dual-purpose outing. In addition to our three-wheelers, we would also cart along six crab rings and, for bait, a supply of frozen fish heads from our numerous fishing expeditions. On arriving at Boxcar, we would hop on our three-wheelers and ride to our hearts' content for 15 to 20 minutes. Then we would head south about 200 yards to the train **trestle** bridge and check our crab traps.

Most days, we rarely caught more than two or three legal Dungeness crab. At about one pound each they made for a great Crab Louis appetizer for dinner. But we would always haul in a couple of hundred purple rock crabs over our three- to four-hour dual-purpose excursion. We kept that many because at that time there was no limit on rock crab, which had been deemed pests and were beginning to compete with the **indigenous** Dungeness.

Mind you, most people wouldn't bother to even keep one rock crab. The sea critters didn't have any measurable, retrievable meat, except for what we'd pull from their pinchers, which were huge in relation to their body size. In fact, the rock crab has pinchers two to three inches long, which rivaled a Dungeness crab of twice their body size! Legally, you were supposed to take the whole crab, and would be fined if you just took the pinchers and threw the remainder back.

This potential money drain deterred us from being inhumane but we would still take home as many of the rock crabs that John and I could catch. We always brought them home, cooked up a crab feast, and then took the excess rock crabs we didn't eat and rotor tilled them into my Mom's huge garden. (That was the little-known secret to our excellent fertilizer.)

On one of our more memorable outings we stopped at the end of the bridge. After dismounting our three-wheelers, it was our custom to put our ears to the rail track, to make sure that no trains were coming. If we detected no vibrations, we were easily clear to walk down the track itself as the vibration method is a surefire way to tell if a train is coming, long before you can see it.

Once we got out to where our six lines were tied up on the trestle, we would begin the process of hauling up our crab pots. We would then bring back our catch and put them in the cooler, which sat in the back of my retired Weyerhaeuser firewood truck. Then we would again hop on our three-wheelers and start the whole process over again.

One time the bait was fairly well eaten by the crabs since we had been out riding for a half hour. This was actually fairly common, so as usual we had to go back out and restock our traps. After we had accomplished that small task, John happened upon a piece of paper, which he promptly began crafting into a paper airplane. Looking down, I found a Budweiser bottle cap, and said, "I'll race you!" (I knew full well that the cap would jet out faster than any paper plane would go.)

Now, John was about as competitive a person as you will ever meet. I enjoyed playing golf with him, or getting into basketball games such as horse with him. Even though he usually won these contests, he was the type to push you to your limits. Over the years I had found that he was actually forcing us both to become better at almost anything we were doing, sporting or otherwise.

Rising to the occasion and tipping the contest in another direction, he asked, "Which do you think will go farther, Eddy, the plane or the bottle cap?" I grinned, and replied, "Well, if you want to make our normal dollar wager, I'll go with the airplane." No way!" he boomed authoritatively. "Bets off," he added, eyeing the landscape in front of us.

Tossing the plane, it made a remarkable flight--a good 75 feet--and then suddenly lost momentum and began a quick death spiral 35 feet down into the salty water. Meeting the challenge I placed the cap between my thumb and middle finger, and let it go with a snap. Under normal circumstances, the metal crown would make it 40 to 50 feet.

However, at that moment, a slight wind came up and lofted the cap. It danced on the air, and just kept going—50 feet, 75 and then, at about 100 feet, it started fading out of view. We stood there, dumbfounded, for a few minutes, peering over the horizon. We were half expecting to see the bottle cap at the very least splash down or boomerang back to us for a redo.

Sheepishly, I looked over at John, and blurted, "Boy, I'm sure glad you didn't take that bet!"

Moral of the story: The race doesn't always go to the obvious, but that's still the way to bet.

9
Charley Horse!

Sherman Gardiner was a husky 88-year-old Native American Indian. If you ever saw his garden you would realize that some people truly resemble their birth names. **Nestled** between his home and the apartments he owned on the other side of the block, was his **botanical** pride and joy. Sherman's hobby, growing top-quality **epicurean** delights, was primarily limited to a few specialties: tomatoes, hot chili peppers, onions, garlic and cilantro.

For those of us living in close proximity, Sherman's garden made for a welcoming **sanctuary** of sorts, especially after a punishing 7-mile run. My favorite steed to rest upon was really a flat bench situated between two trees facing a prime view of Southern Oregon's majestic Siskiyou Valley. This spot almost always **elicited** the sense of granting a brief **respite** from reality; it was here where I had often stopped to reflect, before hitting the shower.

Once, in the fall, I had the good luck of witnessing the first dark storm of the season, from precisely that mount. The peculiarity of this particular snowstorm was the warm front that it was slowly conquering as it moved and deepened. On the developed west side of the valley, a veritable blizzard was dumping heavy snow. Turning my head to the east 180 degrees yielded a profoundly different picture. The undeveloped, **pristine** grass-covered hillside I had left only minutes earlier was still warm, sunny and calm. It was on this particularly hot October afternoon while relaxing after an intense, **interval** style, speed workout, tragedy struck. The bite of a **mythical Charley Horse** pierced into my right leg and then, without warning, another clamped on to my left. Perhaps two beasts of burden had sunk their teeth into me simultaneously, to share in a meal-sized hors d'oeuvre. The pain was so **excruciating** that I let out a scream and fell off my favorite four-legged steed backwards, and was benched to the ground.

Hurrying over from his garden, Sherm, as we all called him, looked visibly shaken by my spectacle. "Eddy, what's wrong?" he cried out. "Charley Horse," was the only thing I could **stammer** out in my **distress**. "Hold on," he replied. "I've got a guaranteed cure in the house."

Trying without success to straighten out my legs, I shouted out, "Don't worry, Sherm, I'm not going anywhere."

An agonizing three minutes later, Sherm reappeared at my side with a bottle of Schweppes **tonic water** and commanded me to "guzzle four gulps of this stuff." I was in pain, but I also knew that tonic water had a terrible taste. I looked at him like he was nuts. I knew that the tonic's bitter bite would be exceedingly unpleasant, but I still had to ask how it would do any good. "The **quinine** in the tonic water that makes it tastes so bad," he explained, "is what relaxes the muscles. Besides, it works. Trust me."

Whether it was merely a matter of timing, or the power of suggestion, or a chemical imbalance in my system, my muscles released. Within a minute of downing the **vile** tasting liquid, the pain was gone. Thanking Sherm, I asked him how he had learned about the cure. A slow laugh framed by a grin came over his face as he **recounted** a story about how his high school track coach, Jack, had always carried a bottle of quinine in his jacket pocket around with him. When the inevitable casualty of "horse play" dropped beside the track, Jack would place a drop on the victim's tongue. Getting to my feet, I started, instinctively, to hand back the bottle of tonic water to Sherm. He chuckled, and said, politely, "No thanks, Eddy, You will need it again, long before I do!"

Moral of the story: Never look a gift horse in the mouth.

10
Compound Bow Hunting Class 101!

When I was in junior high school, our **curriculum** enabled us to take electives outside the three R's, and I was fortunate enough to have taken a class called Hunters Safety. In that class we learned the usual safety tips:

1) Never point a gun, loaded or unloaded, at anyone.
2) There are absolutely no absolute rules for ammunition, i.e., they can explode when dropped, have a slow burn and easily go off 15 or more seconds after a misfire, and are not governed by any hard and fast rules.
3) Always set your gun down when going over or under a fence.

4) Don't hold your finger on the trigger until you've decidedly committed to pull the trigger.
5) Don't keep a loaded gun in your truck.

We also learned a lot of other nifty skills, such as fishing knots, tying flies, wild game calls, field dressing shortcuts and camouflage techniques. Our teacher, to whom we had given the nickname Domino, also instructed us in other essentials: quartering elk, hunt-related personal **hygiene**, small game tricks, hypothermia survival and fire essentials. Most importantly, he taught us common sense and common courtesy.

Two years after I had taken the class I found myself in full "cammo" deep in the woods. Now, this was not your ordinary Army Surplus camouflage but rather an outfit of my own making. I realized that I needed something better than the traditional flat sleek fabric broken up by woodsy print. I wanted the impossible, something which would not show the **silhouette** of a man.

I had started with well-worn basic tan colored pants commonly known as "cords," and opted for larger corded thick ridges, which would be good for providing depth. Next, I used brown Rit dyes and excessively boiled down leaves as a base for drawing outlines of big bark branches and leaves, which made for a good **collage**. On top of that I had sewn on several pieces of brown and green ½-inch rope, resembling small branches, along with hundreds of scraps of cut-out cloth. These green and brown "leaves" were securely but loosely attached so that they would **rustle** in a soft breeze. I could sit down Indian-style in the middle of any field, and most people would just think I was just a **rogue** bush.

In addition to the visual effect of the apparel, which I only wore while hunting, I attempted to authenticate the scent of the woods. I stored the outfit in cardboard boxes, one inside another, that contained deer scent, skunk scent, crushed leaves and fir needles, and clayish dirt all wrapped up in an old deer skin with a couple of rolls of paper towels to absorb any excess moisture.

Whether any of this helped as an odor masker for human scent I am not sure. But from a high school sophomore's perspective, it was good enough for me. The theory I was following from class was that it is better for the hunter to have natural smells than to go out freshly lathered in Irish Spring soap and Allspice after-shave, if you catch my whiff.

One day I was out testing my survival skills--sporting my full-cammo outfit and carrying a topographical map, binoculars, my .38-caliber special and the works for scouting. I was just walking the tree line of a very large meadow bordered by a cliff with a stream running around it, when I heard a rifle shot emanating from 50 yards ahead of me. Out of the corner of my eye I caught a glimpse of something very large falling off the cliff and into the very shallow stream that ran all the way around the base of it. A couple of poachers had just shot a cow elk, which had evidently died and stumbled off the path.

I didn't want to move, but I had to see more to decide

what my next move would be. To my surprise, I discovered that the poachers were a school classmate, Greg, and his father. It made sense, in a way, as I had heard that Greg's dad had been out of work for over a year because of declining timber sales.

I just sat and watched in the bush, and to my **chagrin**, my problem of how to get an elk out of this rugged valley was being solved before my eyes. The pair blew up two inflatable rafts with a bellows-like foot pump and pulled out their walkie-talkies. Then Greg took off and headed down the stream.

A few minutes passed before his father pushed off, in a much larger rubber raft, on which he carted the now gutted elk. I thought to myself, "Wow, what a great way to get meat out of a totally inaccessible area!" I also decided to come back a week later and explore the stream.

It turned out that I didn't have to postpone the visit. Because I had always been a cross-country runner, I had made it back to my old GMC truck after 30 minutes of fast hiking. A few miles down the dirt road, I saw Greg walking in front of me, toward the only bridge that crossed the stream. Being cordial but playing innocent, I stopped after crossing the bridge and said hello, and asked Greg if he wanted a ride. He declined, and told me that he was just out for a walk. "I only live a half-mile down the road," he said, "in that white house near the stream." To keep the conversation going, I told Greg that I was scouting for the upcoming bow season and had to get home myself. "I live about eight miles from here, next to the golf course," I said, adding that I had better move on it because I was almost late for dinner.

Over the next two years before I had turned 18, I had managed to pull out two cow elk from the same spot with my bow, using a tree and my cammo for cover. But I had failed miserably in getting any bulls. Greg's dad had found work in Idaho, and I hadn't seen another hunter in this spot for two years. It was time to revise my strategy, I thought.

My mission this time, on a warm late summer evening, wasn't just to check out the **lay** of the land. It was a six-point Roosevelt bull elk that I had spotted over the countless hours of sitting in the three tree stands I had installed. I had constructed them out of real tree branches varying in height from 40 to 60 feet above the heather that surrounded the meadow's **perimeter**.

It was high in the trees that I discovered my mistake. In my scouting expeditions, I had learned that the stream and the cliff forced all game to traverse a steep downward path on one end of the cliff. This was the only way in or out for more than two miles, except for a thickly dense quarter-mile-across stand of woods, which only led to another steep-walled valley that met the stream at its bottom.

It turned out that my trigger fingers on my compound bow were to blame for not getting a bull elk. I had sat and watched and camped out for weekends at a time and found that the cows always came down first, followed by the spike and then, after 20 to 30 aggravating minutes, the six-point would finally descend.

One late afternoon which just happened to be the last weekend before rifle hunting season, I had gotten into position at about the time the cows were starting to come down. My location, nestled up against an old, deformed Madrone tree, was superb. The reason for this roost was the physical attributes of this particular tree. The deep green leaves and thin dark orange-red bark matched my cammo extremely well. Also, on one low-lying branch, I discovered the perfect mount--particularly large, and in the shape of an upturned man's arm. The elements had ravaged, and permanently roughened the normally slick sheen. This seat was probably formed by game trampling by while it was young, since it was growing so close to the trail.

From this perch, I could sit in plain view on one of the larger branches, with my feet resting on the ground. This spot was ideal, as it was situated fewer than 20 yards from the **vertex** of the cliff and the stream, where all game had to cross. It was also an easy shot to hit the kill zone since it was less than 12 feet across the stream. In fact I found that my smooth pulling, orange **Recurve** bow matched the form and function of this **Madrone** site better than my compound bow. As much as I appreciate compound bows, their **cantilevers** tend to be a bit jerky on the draw, which is not healthy when a 1,200-pound elk is only a few feet away from you.

Sitting motionlessly, I heard something behind me coming down the tree line. I moved my head slowly, like a praying mantis, with my arrow in its notch ready to fire with a single fluid pull on the string. Then I saw a complete idiot ahead of me, a middle-aged man who ostensibly had no hunting experience at all and was walking through the brush at a brisk pace.

He was whistling, rustling the brush, and to top it all off had an arrow notched as if he was seriously thinking he would find something to shoot. I just sat there in disbelief, watching him edging closer and closer to me. When he was less than a foot away, I bellowed, "Boo!" The guy jumped two feet into the air and dropped his bow!

When he had finished shouting obscenities at me, I asked him what he was doing. "Hunting," he replied curtly. "What for?" I asked, reminding him that he had already alerted every deer within two miles that a human was out and about. "After all, I spotted you more than a quarter-mile away," I said, "and don't forget that deer, elk, bears and cougars all have sense of smell and hearing that's far superior to ours." They can catch your scent from a mile away very easily.

He then became indignant. "There are no cougars out here!" he barked threateningly. I pulled out my trusty .38 in full view, and said, "Why else would I risk a big ticket by having this thing on me while bow hunting, if I didn't know there were cougars out here?"

Clearly realizing the folly of his argument, his demeanor changed. Backing off and profusely apologizing at the same time, he walked away. He really changed his tune but he wasn't whistling this time.

Moral of the story: Even the best-made plans of your life can and will occasionally go wrong due to circumstances beyond your control.

11
Convoy

Spending the weekend at my buddy Tod's house always meant going to Mass on Sunday. This really didn't matter to me much, as my upbringing had been Lutheran, which is fairly closely related to the Roman Catholic Church in many ways. In fact, in those days my parents were just glad that I was still going to church at all, so there was no objection on their part.

One Sunday morning in June, after attending services at Saint Christopher's Church, we stopped at the local shopping mall. The traditional routine was a mad dash across the parking lot to the local Dunkin' Donuts coffee house for a sugar fix. It was probably kind of fun for onlookers to see those four brothers--Tod, Craig, Brian and

Brent--and I all sprint across the lot. Tod always won of course, because, well, he always had the money. After their parents, Ellie and Bob, emerged with the groceries from the Safeway store, we were on our way back to their house.

The six-mile stretch of Highway 101 towards Hauser, Oregon, was long but fairly straight. I had been down this section of road hundreds of times, and by **virtue** of its familiarity, was nodding off in the back seat of the early-1970's Volkswagen bus. The other reason for my **lassitude** was that I was still tired from having stayed up late with Tod the night before. We had been up to our greasy elbows installing a 1600-cc VW engine in his yellow **sand rail**, for running up and down the sand dunes.

That's how it came to be that my eyes were closed and I wasn't exactly in tune with the four other boys' conversation or the banter transpiring between their parents. But I was aware enough to detect an odd and troubling and unpleasant smell permeating the air. Opening up my eyes in alarm, I asked in a loud voice, "What smells like gas?" Suddenly realizing that my outburst wasn't made in reference to **methane**, everyone in the vehicle looked around and acknowledged my alarm.

Someone—I think it was Brent--said, "Hey look. It must be coming from that VW bus in front of us."

Sure enough it was. There was a small but visible drip coming out of the spot where the rear engine was located. After watching this drip spot the highway for about a quarter-mile, we--that's the collective we--the few people "on board" who actually knew a little about engines hotly debated and surmised that the culprit had to be a crack in the gas line. So even though we were about to pass our intended exit, the **consensus** was, in Bob's view, that is, that the decent thing to do was to warn the vehicle's inhabitants that their luck was about to run out.

Forgoing our exit, Bob waited until we were in a safe area to run parallel with the ailing VW in the oncoming lane. Finally, an opening in the opposing flow of traffic allowed us to edge up beside them. As we approached, all seven of us pointed downward in unison, with our index fingers, trying to indicate the problem. In response, the fellow travelers, who sported colorful clothing and truly beautiful hair, all pointed back at us in **ornithological** sign language. Their six birds let us know, in no uncertain terms, that they didn't want our help. Slowing down and pulling off to the side of the road, Bob was by this time **fuming**, as he waited for cars to pass so that we could safely turn around and go home.

Ellie was the first to speak. Looking back at us all, she said, "Well, boys, at least we *tried* to do the right thing. Then Bob took his turn. He slowly turned his head back toward us, smirking in the manner of someone who's becoming more outraged by the minute, and **facetiously** said, simply, "I hope this teaches you all a lesson, boys. Does anyone have a match?"

Moral of the story: Use your best judgment when dealing with strangers.

12

Crater Lake Scare

I t was one of those rare **occasions**--I had about a month off before the start of my sophomore year of college and no firm plans for the immediate future. I had gone up to Ashland early to find an apartment, and somehow managed to find a place that would **accommodate** both my Chevy Cavalier station wagon, and my KZ 650 touring bike. With nothing better to do, I decided to pack up my Lowe Alpine Pack and trusty sleeping bag and take the motorcycle up to Crater Lake for the weekend, and get in a few good runs as I was on the SOSU cross country team.

The drive from Ashland to Crater Lake National Park on a bright summer day, astride a motorcycle blessed with decent power, is something I highly recommend to anyone who has riding experience. If you are of the lifelong-hiker persuasion and interested in making a week of it, or are looking for a summer vacation of a lifetime, there is a vast array of interesting points along the way. I mention this now, as I wish to remind people that Crater Lake is Oregon's only National Park.

My interest in the area begins with the hiking trails in and around the Umpqua National Forest which are many and varied. My favorite is the Mount Thielsen trail. It is a very nice hike, or run, in my case. That is, until the last 200 feet, which is very steep terrain and is a stretch that could almost be classified as a technical climb. Another nearby area I savor is Diamond Lake, which offers numerous relaxation features--camping, boating, swimming, fishing, mountain biking, horseback riding and wildlife viewing, to name just a few. Of course these trails, in and of themselves, would have **potentially** been another day trip or even weekend adventure for me, but my goal was to do a couple of good trails on Crater Lake.

Upon reaching the lodge I waltzed in to the gift shop and then hoofed it upstairs to the lounge, which has marginally better food than the cafeteria and possesses an actual view of the lake, which the cafeteria does not have. To my surprise, I found my high school chess club friend, Marvin, drinking a beer and eating pizza. Approaching him from a 45-degree angle just out of his **peripheral** vision, I asked, in a slightly elevated tone of voice, "Hey, how do I get one of those pointing to a bottle of Budweiser?"

He gulped as he looked up, clearly startled, and even

more surprised to see me then I was to see him. After the initial moment of eye-popping shock, he replied, "Well, Eddy, you have to work here, you have to know and be friends with Dale, the food manager, and you absolutely have to play chess."

I laughed, shook his hand, and said, "I'll take you up on the chess game, but I don't think I'll be working here anytime soon." As he started setting up the game pieces, he said, offhandedly during the normal course of conversation, that one of the dishwashers had quit the night before. Invitingly, he added that the manager was desperate to find someone to take over the main lodge restaurant duties. When I asked Marvin why I would want to work for minimum wage for the rest of the season, he gave me three good reasons: The concession's manager, Bob, almost always wrote glowing letters of recommendation for anyone who stayed the whole season; he gave employees multiple copies of those recommendations on the last day of the season; and he always welcomed back past employees—giving them first pick of the good jobs. "Hmm," I thought, this is sounding better by the minute.

As luck would have it, Bob sauntered up when we were just a few moves into our game. After providing him a brief introduction and a verbal work history, I urged him to call Gino's Pizza in North Bend, Oregon, and ask for Jim, the owner.

He disappeared in to the back room, and in less than 10 minutes, he was back with paperwork in hand and an offer for me to spend the next three weeks as a dishwasher. He chuckled when he reported Jim's response, which was to ask if I wanted to come back to work there. That was amusing, as it had been four years since I had worked there. So as far as Bob was concerned, I was not only hired, I was to report to work at 8 p.m., a mere four hours later.

Wow, room and board paid for in Oregon's only national park—that's one gig that would be hard to pass up! The only bad part was what Bob had neglected to tell me: the other dishwasher had quit at noon.

I was **nonplussed**, for the most part. I'm a little bit of a workaholic by nature, and I generally accepted all of the overtime anyone ever tossed my way. The rest of the crew appeared to accept me almost immediately. After all, I was a friend of Marvin's; I was mostly laid back in the off hours, and a good worker, to top it off.

The only downside I could see was that the job would seriously cut in to my summer break and hiking time. On the plus side, many of the park **personnel** readily and happily shared their secret hikes and tips on cool spots that most people never get to see. The challenge would be a creative one--how to get in some good-quality hikes, given what promised to be a punishing work schedule.

This challenge resulted in some interesting **logistics** at times. One such time, at 12 midnight, I had decided to start out for some seemingly unusual falls. I had found an obscure statement on one of my old outdated trail maps from the 1950's. This particular map was just one of many which I had purchased years before at a garage sale. It indicated that there was a stream of water emerging from the middle of a **pumice** desert. It was circled in red with a note scribbled on the side of the map proclaiming, "Beautiful--visit again sometime."

My plan was to start my outing after work. Tom, a waiter at the main lodge, and I, were the only civilized individuals around—which, translated in these parts, means people who showered before going to bed. When I told him my plan for the night he looked at me **incredulously**. "Are you crazy? It's already midnight."

I explained that I was going to make the trip via the Pacific Crest Trail. Furthermore was only telling him, so that someone would know about where I was headed in the event I didn't come back. Noting that the walk back from the lodge to our barracks was aglow with a full moon, he reluctantly agreed that I was only slightly crazy and would notify the proper authorities if I didn't show up for work the next day.

After jotting down the approximate location of the trailhead and telling Tom the exact time I was expecting to return, I took off. I decided to coast the seven miles down to the trailhead, hoping to conserve gas. I turned on my light, but it was so bright out that the gesture proved almost unnecessary. Normally, I would have been concerned about my battery being drained by the headlight, but it was brand new, and in addition this bike had a kick start, so I decided it was needless to worry at that point.

Eddy Ivy

On arriving at the trailhead, I had to pull away a few branches to get my motorcycle out of the main view of the road and behind some small bushes. That might strike people as a bit **paranoid**, but the truth is that there's no reason to leave a bike out in the open, in the middle of nowhere with day traffic passing by.

Fortunately, I found an ideal "parking" place--a flat rock about two feet in diameter and level with the ground. I felt relieved that I could use the full engine stand instead of just the kickstand. After locking the steering column and conducting a brief flashlight check of the area and the view from the road, I decided that no one could easily discover where my bike was.

Convinced that my bike was secure, I started off down the dark trail. It was surprisingly light, after my eyes became accustomed to the surroundings. The patches of light blazed, almost like sunbeams, and I could literally see the Pacific Crest Trail markers nailed into trees, despite their lofty placement—12 feet to 15 feet high on account of the winter snow.

After the **initial** climb, the trail leveled out, and I casually checked the front straps on my backpack. At that time I didn't have a firearm, so my trusty whistle and my 12-inch **Bowie**-style buck knife, attached to the front of each strap, sufficed as protection against any unforeseen threat, two-legged or otherwise, I might encounter. I knew from experience that wild game used man-made trails quite extensively at night, as the human-maintained variety are essentially highways in comparison to game trails. Though

I felt fairly secure in the park, these two items I had brought provided me more or less with an extra sense of security.

The trail proved steeper in the beginning than I had judged. After I had trekked an estimated two miles, I was beginning to feel a little bit insecure. The urge to check my **ancient** map with my blinding scuba light was becoming overwhelming, but rather than giving in to the urge to use my halogen bulb and risk **dilating** my eyes, I decided to try to use the moonlight alone.

I was pleasantly surprised to find that I could read the map readily in such cover. Any one of the stray moonbeams filtering through the fir tree branches was more than enough to read the tattered map. Relying on the **contour** elevation lines, I **deduced** that I was on track but somehow sensed that I just might be kidding myself that I was the modern-day equivalent of a Great White Hunter. However, the landmark I sought--a flat, circular meadow at which two trails intersected at 90-degree angles--was **critical**. I had to turn left in the center. Because the map was more than four decades old, I didn't know if the trees would be grown in. That alone could possibly **thwart** my mission, as I had already passed what had appeared to be many such trails.

Fortunately my fears proved unfounded. A few minutes later I came to the clearing, which was far larger than the map's suggested 150 yards in **diameter**. My relief was short lived; as soon as I stepped out of the darkness of the trees, I felt a new presence—one that I had never really sensed before in any situation of my life. By the time I was about 10 yards into the grassy **oasis**, an uneasy feeling began to overtake me.

The stillness of the night was gone and had been replaced by movement. I could not see anything except movement. Nothing was visible in the bright moonshine though I could see everything, and it was all still, but still moving. No lurking shadows along the tree line, no movement in the grass. Not a blade of grass was bending, yet movement was all around me. It was dry, still and silent except for the movement.

I cautiously unsnapped my knife and began to clench it. You know that feeling, being scared of something when you know something is wrong, but knowing, too, that you just can't quite put your finger on it. I proceeded to the cross the trails made and decided that if I was going to leave this world at least I would go out like Jesus on a cross. Questioning my sanity at this point, I lowered into a crouching position.

Arriving at the crossroads I stopped and spun around, once, twice, three times, knife in hand and peering anxiously toward the tree line. Now it seemed clear that since the time I had stepped into the circular field, the movement I was seeing in my mind intensified around the edges of the meadow. I froze, raised my knife, checking to make sure my sleeping bag was protecting my neck and listened, waiting and watching—for I knew not what.

In my wanderings over the years, I have witnessed two

cougars, many brown bears and a few **feisty** small but potent striped kitties that I wouldn't care to cross paths with, frankly. Yet, I still didn't have a clue of what was about to transpire, on this night in this place, or why my senses were acting as they were to an unknown adversary.

After at least three agonizing minutes, I looked up at the moon, and to my surprise—and utter relief, ultimately--I saw two huge owls circling over my head a mere three or four feet out of reach. As soon as I spied them, one took off and clenched a mouse that was crossing the path about 25 feet south of me. With a relieved sigh, I had to laugh--those turkeys were using me merely as a decoy to flush out mice. What nerve!

I recovered, got my bearings, and made my way to the **cascading** falls about a half-mile away due South according to my compass. I was just about to set up camp near the falls when I felt uneasy again. This time I took out my high powered waterproof scuba flashlight and turned it on. To my amazement, everything around me was lush and brilliant green. Evidently, it was the humidity that had had triggered my unrest this time.

Looking at the falls gently cascading down its 20-foot staircase, I saw a fine mist that emanated in a semi-circle of about 35 feet in diameter before evaporating. The stream itself was very small and contained water horsetail ferns. Along the banks there were the classic wood horsetail ferns, which are sometimes called puzzle grass because you can pull the sections of the plant apart and put them back together again.

Eddy Ivy

Of course, there were other green lovelies in this micro-climate--like the maidenhair spleenwort, rigid bracken ferns, sword ferns galore and a velvet covering of moss that would have made for a nice soft mattress. It was so unlike the pumice desert around it that I pulled some words of wisdom out of one of my scuba buddy's stories. Rich had been on cross-country tour of the United States on his 10-speed bike when he stopped for the evening at a nice rest area. He threw out his sleeping bag on the lush green grass seemingly in the middle of nowhere. At about 3 a.m. automatic sprinklers came on despite no apparent plumbing. I still recall his words, "Eddy, if it's green in the desert, it means it gets watered at night".

I wisely set up camp 30 yards upstream away from the fine mist, and I slept high and dry!

Moral of the story: Learn from the stories of others!

13
Devil Dog

The note on the employee bulletin board read: Free dog to a good home. The picture was worth a thousand words. She was half German shepherd and half Rottweiler with emerald green eyes, and she was just eight months old. I contacted my co-worker, Kristy, who explained why the dog needed a home: She was moving out of her parents' place and into an apartment complex that didn't allow large dogs.

As the dog was still only a puppy, I didn't even think to ask about its **disposition.** Kristy and I made arrangements for her to come over to the house to check out the kind of place that her beloved dog, Lady, would soon be calling home. All seemed to go well; the dog was well behaved and didn't mind being petted, and she seemed to be of good **temperament**.

Like all puppies would, Lady immediately took a liking to my large, grassy and entirely fenced back yard. There also was a narrow runway on the side of the house that led out front, allowing for a large play area for a **rambunctious** pup. While Kristy and I talked inside, the dog lay out on the back porch and eventually took a nap-- which all good dogs do from time to time, and which seemed a pretty good sign to me about the chapter ahead.

Kristy was scheduled to work the afternoon shift, so when things appeared calm she said, "Hey, Eddy, I need to go now," and I headed out to mow the front yard and side yards. After finishing that small task I decided to feed Lady. After I opened the sliding glass door, my sweet little Lady turned into a fang-toothed, blazing-eyed devil. Despite the fact that I had a bowl of food in my hand, she still tried to bite me. Fortunately, she only managed to damage a few hundred freckles.

Using the now empty dish as a shield I walked inside in total shock. The food on the deck was soon gone, and my left-foot Birkenstock sandal had **metamorphosed** into a chew toy. Looking at the slight bruise on my hand, I discovered that tiny bubbles of blood were starting to materialize. I walked to the medicine cabinet and examined my options: **iodine tincture** or **hydrogen peroxide**. As I had a second bottle of peroxide in the bathroom, I **doused** my arm immediately and headed to the local hospital for a **tetanus** shot.

When I returned home, dismayed and becoming more than a bit perturbed I realized that the distinctly unlady-like dog didn't have any water. I hoped, optimistically, that perhaps the small outburst may have been just a small **temper tantrum**, so I filled up her water dish and slowly opened the sliding glass door ajar with the water at her nose level.

My offer of a beverage didn't go over well. Lady started to snarl and gnash her teeth again. Closing the door, my gut instinct told me that there were a host of reasons that Kristy wanted to get rid of this dog—and that her impending move to the apartment might be the least of them.

As I was contemplating my next move, the front doorbell buzzed. Looking up, the reflection of my good buddy Brian's white truck appeared in the window. Opening the door with a smile and smirk, the first thing out of my mouth was, "You are just the man who can solve my small problem."

Escorting him to the back he was taken back when my puppy of a problem started chewing off my aluminum screen on the outside of the door, growling and snapping in her apparent eagerness to get to us. He pulled out his cell phone and dialed. "Hi, sis," he said, when Theresa answered. "Eddy's got a problem that he needs to talk to you about." I had forgotten that Theresa was a police dog trainer, until I started in with the story of the dog.

"Well, Eddy, you have two options—and you probably won't like either one," Theresa said, **somberly**. I eyed

Brian with my questioning look, paused and looked down at the floor, and waited for the bad news. "You can either shoot her now or give her back to Kristy," Theresa said almost matter-of-factly.

"You're right, I don't like either option, because Lady is probably the best-looking dog I've ever seen," I offered, "as Brian here can **attest**. Why can't we try to do something on the behavior side first before going through with one of those options?"

Her response was that even though Lady was still a puppy, she had already fixated on Kristy. As both breeds are bred to be protective, sometimes they will turn vicious on anybody if the master isn't around. She then gave me the very worst-case future picture: "If that dog gets loose and bites someone, or, God forbid, kills a young child, you are going to be liable, Eddy."

That was enough for me. I called Kristy's number and reached her parents, who, as it turned out (surprise, surprise), didn't want the dog back at their house either. I then asked them to have Kristy call me as soon as she got home. The inevitable phone call came. Of course, Kristy was tearful as she stammered, in between gulping sobs, that she couldn't possibly have her dog **euthanized**. I opted for the firm, calm and collected response. "Kristy, you can either come take the dog tonight, or I'm going to have to call animal control," I said, "because I can't even feed her without being bitten."

After her shift ended, Kristy showed up and was happy

to see her dog. Showing her my scars and explaining why I couldn't possibly keep her dog any longer, she apologized and thanked me for trying. I was sad to see the dog go. But sometimes in life, things don't go as well as you plan.

Moral of the story: Don't bite the hand that feeds you.

14
Endangered Species

Deep in the heart of Oregon lies a reservoir named Lake Billy Chinook. It's prized for being one of Oregon's most beautiful recreational destinations. The lake was formed in 1964 when General Electric built the Round Butte Dam. The three rivers that feed the lake make for great fishing, while the two main campgrounds make for a relaxing summer getaway. Topping off the list of amenities is the marina, which rents houseboats, ski boats, and jet skis.

As a member of the Bergfreunde Ski Club, I had the good fortune of spending most of my Labor Day holidays at an annual outing with the club known as the Bergies. It is an all activities, strictly volunteer lead club based in

Portland Oregon. Besides the annual Bergie picnic, the Cove Palisades/Lake Billy Chinook trip had always been my favorite.

The primary attraction of the three-day camping event is top-notch waterskiing in the early mornings and sunbathing in the afternoons. These two activities, along with the lively barbeque dinners, are usually more than enough to suit my fancy. But not for the Bergies. No, these folks go in for major hikes on well-kept trails and up the back side of the nearby world-famous Smith Rock State Park, volleyball games and the nighttime campfires to round out the experience.

One year the holiday weekend weather forecast was rather bleak, so I decided to take along my trusty old canoe. It was quite the conversation starter; my idea for camouflaging the vessel was to cover it first in green base paint and then overspray real sword ferns with a dirt-brown waterproof paint. The effect was both artful and eye-catching. My reason for bringing the craft along was twofold. For one, I had discovered that many of the women in the club happen to enjoy moonlit canoe rides. The second reason was more **mundane**—I'd go fishing if the overcast-weather forecast actually transpired.

The second day of the campout was extremely overcast. The covering layer of **cumulus** clouds was less than 300 feet overhead and resembled the texture of an old favorite worn out sweater. They gathered in a crochet-like weave that allowed a smattering of light to pierce the blanket here and there. This created a silky gray-mesh **dappling** effect on the surface of the water, which makes for perfect fishing conditions. I knew that the threatening look of the clouds and the occasional raindrop would keep most of the normal club activities at bay until the late afternoon, so my schedule was now set.

As I would be fishing on an Indian reservation, I had to stop in at the local marina and purchase a tribal day license. When I asked what I ought to have on hand in the way of fishing gear, and what I might expect to catch for my day's efforts, the cashier offered his full-on prescription for success: "You'll probably limit out at 25 kokanee salmon if you use a wedding ring lure about three or four feet back from a Ford Fender spinner."

I replied, "OK, but what about the lakes famous bull trout?" The fish, which are an endangered species in the rest of the Pacific Northwest, are legal to catch here. The reason for their success is that they have a **voracious** appetite for the plentiful kokanee and as a result produce many trophy-sized fish every year. Needless to say the potential to legally catch an endangered species is a **boon** to the local economy.

The man's eyes challenged me to catch one, and after a huff of a chuckle, he offered this bit of elderly advice. "Well, since you can't use a kokanee, anything that resembles one will be good. But you ought to know, young fellow that they aren't biting today."

Feeling well informed and a bit dismayed, I made my way to the public boat launch closest to the mouth of the meandering and scenic Metolius River, where it empties into Lake Billy Chinook. Not knowing what to expect, I carted along an Igloo cooler lunchbox full of food that had previously, yet conveniently been located in the trunk of my car for emergencies. In the container were extra pop, chips, candy bars, and every conceivable type of junk food that would last 10,000 years in the event of nuclear war.

Next I grabbed my even larger tackle box, and my grandfather's orange trout pole, and was soon on my way to a well-known fishing hot spot about two miles from the public dock. As I was alone, I pushed my colossal tackle box into the nose of the canoe to provide a counterbalancing effect. At 12 inches long and 12 inches deep by two feet wide, and filled with at least one lure of every type I had ever been able to get my hands on, it handily provided a good 25 pounds of needed weight.

Approaching the mouth of the Metolius, the evidence of the hot spot was overwhelming. A **flotilla** of at least 40 odd vessels pressed into tight rows, like sardines in a can. If it weren't for the snags on either side of the lake, I might have been able to walk across the entire span from boat to boat.

I didn't have an anchor, so my sole option for staying put was to throw a rope around an upright log sticking up out of the water. The nearest boat happened to be piloted by the game warden, who promptly asked me for my license. We were only about eight feet apart, so it was easy to tie the paper on the end of my pole and simply fork it over. He laughed at my gesture, and after looking at the license, said, "Good luck. We haven't caught anything here all day." It was only 8 in the morning, so the fishing day was indeed very young, I knew. I confidently replied, "Well, I have at least eight hours worth of food and a couple hundred types of lures, so I guess I'm set!

The fish weren't biting, so I decided to take a few myself by getting a early start on lunch. The ham sandwich, compliments of the Bergies, was a bit too cheese-laden for my taste. That I remedied with the perfect antidote: a side of hot canned **authentic** Mexican jalapeno peppers from my survival box.

After my encounter with the spicy chilies, I had to wipe my brow before taking a look at my tackle box. Dipping into a well-chosen niche in the side drawer, I carefully extracted my favorite lure of all time, the one ounce black and silver rooster tail. Why not? I thought. The rest of the **armada** was in deeper water and only my nimble sleek canoe was able to navigate the logs of death near the shore. I paddled about five feet closer in so that I could tie off to a sturdier old log, thereby boosting my comfort and adding support.

I began casting. About 40 casts later, a gentle whirr of the reel signaled that I either had a bite or was about to lose my favorite lure to a snag. Coming to attention I sat upright and set the hook by pulling up sharply. The realization that I had a fish on and not a clump of algae, log or piece of debris, brought rousing cheers from the otherwise **sedentary** anglers. The **ensuing** fight delivered a spectacular show for those unlucky saps, who were sitting in their motorized speedboats drinking beer and pretending to fish. I had never had a fight like this one in my life. Fortunately the test on my line was 8 pounds of overkill.

The first thing I noticed was that my boat was still tied to the log. This was good and bad. The good aspect was that it added some support. The bad aspect was that I had to force the fish to not get near the log, **lest** it get tangled up and snap the line. After the fish ducked under my canoe the first time, I had to stand up. That was a bad move. I almost fell in, and quickly found that I could stand up for a second or two, but the fish was big enough to make me lose my balance from the force of his pull. A single poorly timed stance would send me and the contents of my canoe to the bottom.

At first I was just frustrated. The wily fish would go under the boat and back again. By letting the line out a little when he went under, I could whip the tip of my pole around the end of the canoe and work him back in. Side to side, he tried to get away; he must have been intelligent, because he soon decided to head to the front. This was even more unsettling, as not only my Igloo lunch box but also my tackle box and net were smack in the way—not to mention the canoe's two stationery crossbeams. My movements were erratic, as I was matching the fish's darting attempts to get free.

The laughter from the **peanut gallery** was also becoming unnerving, to say the least. Finally I started to wear him down, and fortunately, I succeeded in wrestling him in close enough to net him. Fortunately or unfortunately, as the case may have been, the game warden, a large Native American man, was still in the boat right next to me.

"Nice show, but you'll have to let him go, Great White Hunter," he pronounced with a **sardonic** laugh. "I can see from here that your fish isn't the minimum 24 inches." My homemade tackle box was precisely 24 inches long, so I knew he was right. Geez, I thought. If only the fighter had another inch on him, I'd have had another notch on my box.

I gently released my hoped-for dinner back into the lake, and instead of taking off in a shot like most fish would, it headed slowly straight toward the game warden's boat. The fish appeared to be a little dazed by its slow movements, but was none the worse for wear.

A mere few seconds later, we were suddenly startled by a huge splash. Something the size of a bowling ball had just landed next to my boat. After the spray had landed on me and the warden it became apparent that an **osprey** had sunk its **talons** into the back of my fish. Wet and startled, he and I looked at each other and the battle now unfolding, just as the previous battle had ended.

It was an amazing spectacle, the likes of which I'd not seen in many years. The osprey was thrashing about in the water next to my boat. At first I was unsure what was going on, as I had never witnessed predator and prey in action so up-close. It finally dawned on me that the osprey was in trouble. I had learned once in an ornithology class that ospreys have a locking feature in their talons that can kill them if they latch onto a fish that is too big for them to carry off. If the fish is big enough it can actually pull the bird down and drown him.

Watching this life and death struggle was exciting but almost too disturbing for us to handle. But we didn't intervene. The bird would flap his wings and almost get out of the water; then the fish would thrash and pull him back down. The scene repeated a half-dozen times or so until the fish finally gave up, limp with exhaustion, and the osprey finally got out of the water, nearly two minutes later.

Slowly and tentatively, the bird flew out over the lake about two feet over the water, as if struggling to gain altitude. Fortunately, he must have caught a breeze and the updraft pulled him up to about 30 feet in the air, before he turned back and started heading toward us. We were startled again, as he headed straight for us and then landed in a tree directly overhead. Then we saw the nest!

Looking up at the game warden, I laughed, and said, "At least someone is going to have a good fish dinner tonight!"

Moral of the story: A fish in the talon is worth two in the sea.

15

Goop In A Glass Jar

When I arrived in Great Falls, Montana, as a second-grader, the landscape was a new experience, to say the least. After spending kindergarten and first grade living on the shores of Lake Washington in Seattle, Great Falls seemed **arid** and **stark**. I was used to walking **amid** a lush diversity of towering trees and playing in **verdant** undergrowth. My new city's predominant play structure was the mighty Poplar, which does very well in that climate but simply cannot compete with the grandeur of the Douglas fir.

Of course the first thing that I wanted to see as a kid was the **renowned** water falls, so on my second evening there my father took me down to the Missouri river. As we approached the hydroelectric power plant, he pointed to the structure, and then pronounced, "There are the falls, Eddy!"

Puzzled, I looked up at him and asked, "But where are the falls?" He explained that the explorers Lewis and Clark had spent a month going around the falls on their historic expedition, and that now the falls had been dammed up to produce electricity.

Explaining the need for power was easier for my dad than addressing my next question, which was, "Why did we have to leave Washington?" He explained that the **kite factory**, which I knew was his slang for The Boeing Company, wasn't selling enough airplanes and had to lay off thousands of workers. He emphasized how fortunate he felt to have landed an instructor's job at the Montana State Auto College in Great Falls. He also said that he was happy to be back in Montana, where he had grown up as a boy and where he still had many friends.

Being the new kid on the block with no friends in second grade can be tough. And moving into a new place in the summertime is even tougher than during the school year, as there are a lot fewer kids to associate with between June and the start of school in September. In my case, losing a dozen or so playmates was probably more devastating to me than my family had realized. As I was a slightly hyperactive child, having a lot of friends proved a good way to make time fly during the summer. New games, friends, and exciting toys such as walkie talkies and crystal radio kits were the standard fare in Bellevue's garages, if you associated with other engineers' sons. My new home neighborhood didn't appear to even boast kids my age, or so it seemed.

Boredom quickly set in. I discovered that a young boy can only fit 573 grasshoppers into a gallon jar so many times, just for fun, if you know what I mean. The second week in to what I'd come to view as my enforced torture, I met twin brothers who lived up the street about two blocks away. Terry and Torrie were seven years old like me, and both sported **Mohawk**-style hair cuts. It turned out that they had established a little club, and that in order to join the club, prospective members were required to do all sorts of heroic (and/or dastardly) deeds, depending on one's point of view.

With little else to amuse myself, I decided I wanted to join their club they had named "The Injuns." I asked who else was in it. The reply, which, looking back seemed to issue a bit too quickly from Terrie's mouth, was that the other members "were away for the summer." To my seven-year-old mind, I suppose that made sense.

The first day of my initiation included climbing up a tree, then crawling out on a branch far enough to drop on to the roof of a garage, shimmy down a fence on the other side, crawl up an apple tree in an old lady's back yard, and bring back three apples. It all sounded rather elaborate and not particularly smart. I looked at the brothers quizzically, and said, "But geez, guys, why don't we just ask her for the apples?"

"That's not the point, Eddy," they retorted in unison, laughing at me. Since there were so many culls of rotten fruit on the ground, numbering more than 100 by my rough count, I did the deed--while justifying my action by telling myself that the neighbor really didn't care about the apples. Thus, I passed the first test.

The second day of my initiation the test involved jumping off a cliff. It wasn't really a cliff but more of a ledge, in a pit that a bulldozer had made for the basement of a new building that was going up. It was a few blocks from our homes, and was located behind a high chain link fence, which was exciting to **shimmy** under. Winding through machinery, lumber and heavy equipment, we made our way to the construction site.

Looking down 20 feet from the grassy edge to the sandy bottom, I shuddered slightly, and said, "No way." They then assured me that the landing—"It's just sand," they said, cheerfully—would be soft, and added that they'd both done the jump before.

I thought about it, and then decided to "test the waters" myself, by going down to the base to see what the landing was like. The twins were right about the sand, which formed a 45-degree angle up from the base to about 10 feet up the wall.

I made a few test jumps by climbing up the sides to build up my courage. With the fear then somewhat diminished, I was able to attempt the full jump. As it turned out, in the same manner that my test jumps had proved less difficult than I expected, I found I could drop into the angled sand to make the full leap, which softened my ultimate landing. And so the second test was history.

The third day of my initiation involved the so-called "bravery test." At this point, despite my boredom, being pushed around by these guys for their amusement was starting to get old. When one twin would suggest something the other would back him up, and the majority always ruled. To boot, the **banter** was sometimes rude, even between the brothers, and swearing was as much a part of their standard vocabulary as it was their bravado jargon.

Buy this time, I had seriously started to wonder about the existence of the "other members," and my need for friendship was starting to be replaced by my annoyance at the whole scheme of the club. To my mind, the whole exercise was beginning to become an ordeal to be endured, rather than a potential social connection **venue**.

But I followed them, out of curiosity if nothing else, into an abandoned garage. The third test, they announced somberly, was to drink some brownish fluid from an old glass gar sitting on the shelf. Lifting it up and taking a sniff, I decided to turn the tables.

"You go first," I said, eyeing them innocently. "No, Eddy, that's not how it works," Torrie replied.

I bought a little time while I gathered my thoughts, and then replied, "Well, you know, my dad is a teacher at the auto college. He says this kind of stuff can be poisonous."

Looking a bit at a loss for words, the twins glanced at each other quickly and spurted, "Then you can't be in our club, Eddy."

I picked up the glass jar of goop, held it out to the side slightly, and then let it fall to the concrete floor.

"Well, you guys. I guess nobody else can be in your club either," I declared.

Moral of the story: Listen to your parents.

16
Grandpa Art's Fly Fishin' Pole

I had always **coveted** my grandfather Art's fiberglass fly fishing pole. Its color was like the **opaque** icy-white glaze of a pina colada, or the cool gaze that grandpa always gave me whenever I got within a couple of feet of it. It stood invitingly in the corner of the back porch next to an old reed fishing box. He had bought it new around the time when the first fiberglass poles were introduced to the market, in 1946.

For some reason Art just had to buy a Shakespeare Wonderod. I'm sure it didn't cost too much, as he was still fairly newly wed, but still, he had always considered the pole a luxury item, not a toy. Although he hadn't used it in more than 20 years, my grandfather had always responded with a quick and **unequivocal** "No" whenever I tentatively asked if I could, might ever have that pole.

One day, in early November 1971, my grandfather passed away. I was old enough to know that he was never coming back, but young enough not to feel the need to cry. When I was visiting my grandmother about a week later, I happened across the old pole while I was putting out a saucer of milk for the neighbor's cat on the back porch.

I asked, "Grannie Annie, "Do you think I could have Grandpa Art's old fishin' pole?" With a wide smile and red-rimming eyes, she replied, "Well, yes, Eddy. Of course you can. After all, you are my favorite grandson." Then she ventured with a muted chuckle. Of course, I was her only grandson. So her term of **endearment**, and this little ritual of ours, was meant more for amusement value for those listening, rather than a confirmation of my request. After all, she herself had told me on many occasions that I had "better not touch that pole as long as my grandfather was alive."

That was how my grandfather's greatest fear for his prized pole came true. I had a great time with that whip, and I managed to render it totally useless within a couple of weeks. For **sentimental** reasons I kept that pole, and it had its own special place in the garage. For the next eight years, until I turned 17, it collected whatever manner of dust a fishing pole can gather in the rafters of our museumlike garage.

One day in early spring while I was visiting my good

friend, Tod, after a normal day of school, I noticed his younger brother Brian working **meticulously** on a blank fishing rod in their similarly museum-like garage. Hmm, I thought, I wonder if Brian could make me a trout pole out of an old two-piece fiberglass fly rod that's in pretty bad shape. I asked him, and he replied offhandedly, "Sure, Eddy, as long as you pay for all of the accessories."

The very next day I went out and bought the following parts required for the **transfiguration**: stainless steel eyelets, nylon thread, glue for the eye tip, a new cork handle and a special **shellac** to brush over the thread that secures the eyelets firmly in place on the pole. When presented with the **bounty** of items, Brian proved once again that he was one of the nicest guys in the world, when he asked, politely, "How soon do you need it?"

My reply was straightforward. "As soon as you want to go canoe fishing with your brother Tod and me up at Loon Lake," I said, knowing that would be an enticement since Brian didn't have a driver's license, which put the lake out of reach. You see, Brian wasn't always invited, and even the times he was, his parents sometimes didn't allow him to go on excursions they felt might be dangerous. One of those was gold panning on the Sixes River. Tales of miners, who rarely bathed, always carried guns, never cut their fingernails, and had brownish-black teeth, if they had any, were all true. The **nefarious** characters we had come into contact with in those backwoods were larger than life and most were pretty **cordial**, after they got to know you.

The very next weekend my pole was finished. Tod,

Brian, and I loaded up their parent's classic aluminum canoe and headed up to Loon Lake. For the 4 years that I had known Brian, he had always been good at fishing. I think he liked the sport "better than anything else in the world," to quote him **verbatim**. Yes, Brian admittedly could out-fish both Tod and me combined, and it was pretty much expected that he would. We had seen him pull out fish on the first cast using spoons, power bait, rooster tails, wedding rings, worms, cheese, corn--and whatever else was in his lunchbox, for that matter. It was no surprise to either of us that he limited out within a half an hour, and of course we teased him about catching "our fish."

Not long after the Loon Lake trip, I graduated from high school and went off to college. My trusty pole found its way back to its new special spot in a sturdy white capped-off piece of PVC. Over the years I used it once in a while, depending on what kind of fishing I was going to do. But quite frankly, since it had more sentimental value than most of my other 20 or so poles it rarely got used.

Out of the blue, 12 years after we'd left high school, I received a call from Brian. We had stayed in touch and he was calling to see if I wanted to go fishing at Lost Lake in the hills of the Oregon Coast Range. Smiling to myself, I wondered if the invitation had anything to do with my recent canoe purchase. In order to seal the deal, he added, "Hey, the lake was just stocked today!" Brian always knew how to reel in a sucker.

We agreed to go the next day, and set our departure for 4 a.m. from his house. Unfortunately, at the time I was working at one of those jobs where the company pays you just enough so you won't quit, and you work just enough so that they won't fire you. So when overtime was offered the night before, I didn't have much choice but to "sure thing" grudgingly, and stay on. After returning home at 10 p.m., showering and hitting the sack, my dreams were rudely and rousingly disturbed at 4:15 a.m. by a ringing sound in my head that wouldn't go away.

It was, of course, the phone, and as I yanked the mouthpiece off the receiver, I had already started apologizing, stammering that I had forgotten to set my alarm. The fact of the matter was that I had been so tired the night before that I had totally forgotten about the daytrip.

I told Brian that I could be at his house in less than 15 minutes. This is the sort of time when having a **penchant** for **fastidious** organization is a nice trait to possess. The trailer had the canoe, paddles and life preservers, affixed on to and inside the vessel. All I had to do was grab my master fishing tackle box, which weighed about 30 pounds, and the PVC tube that housed my favorite fishing poles. My house was about a mile away from Brian's, so it wasn't hard to accomplish my promised **belated** arrival time. I rechecked the canoe's cinching straps and trailer's hitch connection and we were headed down the road.

Making up time when leaving the **metropolis** of Portland, Oregon, at 4:30 in the morning is a lot easier than in places like Los Angeles, where both Brian and I knew from personal experience that gridlock can happen at any time of the day.

Fortunately, we had calculated the travel time to our destination to account for extra early-morning traffic. As traffic had been virtually non-existent we had ample time to stop for coffee and night crawlers at one of those mom-and-pop convenience stores you often find in the middle of nowhere. We even had time to top off the tank, a smart move since we would be on dirt and gravel roads deep in the woods.

Arriving before anyone else 60 miles outside the city felt like a bit of **redemption** for my having slept in that morning. After unloading the canoe I pulled out two of my poles from the PVC case. One was a lightweight salmon pole and the other was the one that Brian had made—or given new life, as the case was--for me. I then asked him which pole I should use that day, based on his read of the lake. That, of course, was a **baited** question. Not surprisingly, he recommended that I use the pole he had made for me, adding, matter-of-factly, that he had never caught anything over a 14-inch rainbow trout at this lake, which was basically land locked and only had a trickle of a stream going through it.

We paddled out into the middle of the west side of the peanut-shaped body of water. The lake is about the size of two football fields placed end to end. Near to the end of the narrow channel we would be able to effectively work both ends of the lake. The night crawlers weren't doing any good, so we switched to a three-pronged treble hook, baited with an egg-shaped mass of power bait, which can be purchased at most fishing-supply houses.

This **configuration** was working for Brian, but not for me. He caught three rainbows within 20 minutes; I had netted zip! Frustrated (disgusted is more like it), I decided that it was time to pull out my favorite lure of all time: my one-ounce black-and-silver rooster tail. The **swivel** snap I kept on the end of my line always made my lure switching a snap. This brass-and-stainless steel spring-loaded **widget** was a real time saver. In less time than it takes to pull out a thimbleful of doughy fish food, I had opened the locking mechanism and unsnapped my bobber and treble hook and then refastened my favorite lure with a simple squeezing motion of my thumb and index finger.

I cast my line toward shore in what I thought would be a quick smooth move, only to have it catch on my thumb and flip backwards out into the middle of the lake. About two seconds later my mistaken aim produced my first bite of the day. I remember thinking that the fish was coming in without much of a fight, so I was surprised by my friend's **exuberant** exclamation: "You are not going to believe the size of this fish!" I replied, "Yeah, right, Brian. I'll bet it's about a six-incher."

Two seconds later, that fish saw me--and I saw it. Brian wasn't kidding. The beast was nearly three feet long! The next thing I heard was the whirring clicking sound of my reel taking off. This fish was stretching our limited resources and line within minutes. We hadn't thought about needing a net, but we knew that trying to lift the fish into the canoe would have snapped the three-pound line instantly. There was no time to talk we both knew what needed to be done.

While Brian was slowly back paddling us into shore to land the captive on the beach, I was intent on trying to play him out. But he wasn't **cooperating**--at all. He had already managed to take my line all the way out twice and still he wouldn't slow down.

Then, without warning the **inevitable** happened. With a piercing snap, the line broke and the faint web of the last 10 feet of my line sprang back and softly landed on my forehead. Looking up toward my hairline at the end of the wiry stretched line a crooked smile came to my face. Sheepishly, I did the mental calculations and realized that it had been more than 10 years since I had changed the line on that reel—something that should have been done annually.

Laughing, I turned and looked at Brian, and said, "Well, I guess I should have used the other pole!"

Moral of the story: Scheduled maintenance routinely prevents most mechanical failures when emergency performance counts the most.

17

Grandpa Tommy's Orange Trout Pole

Both of my grandfathers, Art and Tommy, were avid fishermen. That is, they fished when they had any time to spare, which **evidently** wasn't much, according to them. The **Great Depression** of the 1930s had taken its toll on leisure time, which was especially scarce for those who had a family to support. Despite that, each of my grandfathers had bought fashionable fiberglass poles that were guaranteed to last a lifetime.

My dad had inherited Tommy's orange trout pole when he was in his late teens, and it was still in **pristine** condition—and I had been **bequeathed** Grandpa Art's once perfect fly rod. As a matter of course, no matter how often I asked, eventually begged, over the years, my dad wouldn't even let me near his father's trout pole, after seeing what I had done to the fly rod while still a child.

One Saturday in the prime of the fishing season when my parents were off running **errands** in town, I spied the orange pole longingly. I was 16, and in all those years I had never seen my dad touch the pole, let alone use it. I thought to myself, "Heck, he'll never know—and they won't be back until at least 6 p.m." I was on my 10-speed in a flash, carrying my small tackle box, which was always ready to go.

The six-mile ride to Gould's lower pond would have been a lot easier and about 20 miles an hour faster on my moped, but I figured I had a lot of time to kill. I actually preferred the bike in some ways; I liked the fact that I could ride upright with both hands free, save gas, and get my exercise in for the day without much effort while riding my bike. The trip to the pond on my 10-speed usually took about 25 minutes there, and just 20 minutes to return, as the route was mostly downhill. And 10 minutes really doesn't matter in the **scheme** of things, when you figure you've got eight hours to burn.

On arriving at the lower pond I encountered an intriguing bunch of people. Six guys, all older than I was and varying in age from 21 to 28, were laughing and carrying on about anything and everything imaginable. Slowing down and hopping off my bike, being careful not to damage the orange pole, I noted the reason for their **jovial** manner. They were drinking hard alcohol out of bottles, which they had tucked into paper sacks. I found this a bit odd since we were 12 miles out of town, but this pond was right on the road and a public thoroughfare so I didn't bother asking about the bags.

Fortunately, I had remembered to bring some lunch, notwithstanding my hasty decision to go fishing. I had brought along a six-pack of Coke and half of a left-over chicken from dinner the night before. Besides giving me **sustenance**, the meat came in handy for bait when things weren't going well. Breaking out my feast of leftovers, one of my colleagues offered to trade me a quarter bottle of rum, for a couple of pieces of chicken and two cokes, as he was leaving anyway.

To join in the **camaraderie** I accepted the offer. I knew that my fellow fisherman weren't really there for the fishing. They were there to get away with the boys and drink, trade the latest jokes, and of course, tell lies.

Now, trying to fit in by drinking isn't always the best policy, especially if you are under age. So it was a good thing, as it turned out, that I had four Cokes left to dilute the rum with for the rest of the day!

Further trying to get with the program, I initially tried everything my **comrades** were using on their lines, even some greasy chicken. The hours began to go by and not a fish was caught. Worse, I was beginning to get bored. (I'm not claiming to be the best fisherman in the world, mind you, but I have always been what you would call a man of action and not a patient bobbing type of guy.) My small tackle box had treble hooks, bobbers, some red spoons, a couple of wedding ring lures, and one of everything else from my large tackle box. Oh, I almost forgot, it contained my favorite weapon of all time: the black and silver one-ounce **rooster tail**.

At about 5 p.m., the sun had started to sink down below the Douglas fir trees enough to make a difference in the lighting of the water. Using this observation as an excuse, I tried all of my spoons and wedding rings and everything left in my arsenal which all failed to do the job. Everything, that is, except the rooster tail. Ready to pack up I stated out loud in a voice loud enough for all to hear, "I'm now going to try my lure of last resort now."

After a couple of long low casts on the upper end of the pond where a small stream fed this man mad pond I was about to call it a day. Then without warning, on my third cast, "bam!" Something grabbed my rooster tail and took off fast, racing across the pond despite my attempts to reel him in. After the first flight, I managed to wrestle what appeared to be a large steelhead, weighing about five pounds, back in to a point where I was able to adjust the **tension** up on my reel before he took off again. This time he was a lot slower in his attempted escape, and was jetting up out of the water in his fury.

Quite by accident, I hadn't checked the reel in my haste when I had left the house. During the day I had discovered that last person whom had used the pole was my Uncle Ralph, who had left 12-pound test when he was fishing for sea bass on the North Bend Jetty. This sucker was not going anywhere except into my frying pan. That I knew.

After adjusting the tension up again, the battle was over; I hauled that land locked salmon's sorry tail up the bank.

Suddenly, in a final, desperate attempt to get away, the fish started flopping down the six-foot embankment. Flipping up into the shape of a crescent moon not once, or twice, but three times he seemed to jump off the grassy bank instinctively towards the water after I had unhooked him. The response from my audience was unanimous and loud, "Get him!" they roared.

I had no choice but to get wet. I ditched the pole, jumped down into the pond to block his escape, and pounded him with all my might on the head three times with my fist. Hauling myself and the hefty salmon, I suddenly had a sick feeling in my gut. I **winced**, squinting **tentatively** as I checked out the pole. It was OK, thank God!

Amid the cheers of my fellow fisher friends, I began to breathe again. Then another sick feeling overtook me when I looked down. My knuckles were bleeding from hitting the fish so hard. Then I glanced at my watch, and panic struck. It was 5:45 p.m., and I was going to be caught red-handed with the orange pole, any way I looked at it.

Using my left hand to grasp the pole, to prevent it from getting bloody, I dug my right hand into the gills of the monster salmon, and was ready to start for home. At about that time the wife of one of my newfound friends on the embankment made a surprise visit. She was just starting to yell obscenities at him for not coming home on time. Then without raising his voice, he pointed at my catch and retorted, "Chill, babe. Look at that kid over there. The fishin's good!"

The six-mile journey passed quickly on my red ten-speed, despite my trail of blood splattering on the pavement and my throbbing arm. I've always been fairly adept at riding without my hands, which came in awfully handy that afternoon. To boot, traffic was especially light; only two cars passed me.

The only 90-degree turn on the entire trip home was at the **tide gate** at the **estuary's** edge. **Navigating** it would be a bit dicey in my current state, I knew. But I managed it without incident and was closing in on home fast when I heard the familiar sound of my dad's International 4-wheel-drive Scout II slowing down. Reluctant to stop, I nervously turned my head toward the Scout. My dad, steely-eyed, was leaning over the steering wheel pointing to the side of the road while trying to look past my mom, who was also looking at me intently.

Blessedly, my mother was the first to speak. In her highest voice, nearly shrill with excitement, she blurted: "Eddy, is that a **salmon**?"

"Yes, Mom. I just caught it in Gould's lower pond—can you believe it?" I exclaimed, in an attempt to perpetuate the happy mood. I added, abruptly, "I'll bet it would cost at least $10 at Safeway!"

Outwardly, my father glared at me, but around the

corners of his mouth a subtle smile was forming. There was a hint, seconds later, that he could hardly suppress the urge to laugh at himself. He knew full well that my mother's favorite food was salmon, and that she would defend me completely, no matter what he had to say at this point. I managed to escape what I thought would be certain doom without a single punishment or penalty I might have incurred otherwise.

From that day on, the orange pole was mine, and I used it whenever I liked.

Moral of the story: Treat your mom like a queen!

18
Happy Father's Day

"Hey, Eddy. What did you do for Father's Day?" Turning my head, I spotted a familiar co-worker, Troy.

I gave him one of those sideways head-tilting gestures, and said, "Hugh," in a quizzical **repartee** tone. "You know, what did you do this weekend?" He repeated again, as he probably thought I was putting him on.

Cornered by his persistence, I blurted out, "Well, I sent my dad a card about a week ago. But I don't have any kids, well, at least none that I know of," I replied, trying to crack a weak joke. "So what did you do?" I asked him, trying to change the frame of reference over to his weekend, which is probably what he wanted to chat about anyway.

"Eddy, you know that just about any time I have a good reason to go fishing, I hook up the boat and go," Troy said. "My son Michael and I went to Battleground Lake--it was **excruciating**.

"What do you mean?" I asked, "Rumor has it that you are one of the better fishermen in this outfit. What could possibly be painful about fishing with your son on Father's day?" I exclaimed.

He explained that his son has a hard time sitting still in the boat for two or three hours, and heaved a heavy sigh. Then, rolling his eyes toward the ceiling as if he was accessing the memory, he said, "I don't mind the talking and fidgeting as much as his inattention to his line and bobber. He probably would have out fished me if he would have set his hook on half of the nibbles he got."

"What's so unusual about that Troy?" I **queried**, trying to pinpoint Michael's age and figuring that he was only about five or six. "I mean, don't all kids need action to keep the interest going?"

I remembered that when I was his age, my parents wouldn't let me touch a fishing pole, let alone be stuck--with my hyperactivity in full gear--in a boat, out on a lake!

Troy, undaunted by my reply, recalled a previous outing with his son. A few months earlier, he said, he had taken Michael out fishing for the first time on a lake. There we were out in the middle for about 25 minutes and hadn't caught a thing. "Of course, you and I know, Eddy, that you need patience to have any success," he continued. "But we had barely baited our hooks when Michael started complaining.

"I, of course, knew this was going to happen, so I started to give him the fisherman's speech: That whenever a boat goes by it spooks the fish for a while so you need to be quiet." That did the trick for awhile, Troy explained, until a large diesel rig pulled up about 20 yards offshore. "I looked over at this truck making a lot of noise, and then I half realized what was going on," he continued.

At that point, even I was confused. "**Pray tell**, what is going on, Troy? I'm really not following the story very well," I blurted in mild frustration. "Just what does a truck have to do with the story?"

Smiling, Troy now knew that he had me hooked. Pretending to be annoyed, he changed his vocalization and **rebuked** me. "Just hold on, Eddy, and quit interrupting, and I'll tell you," he said, grinning austerely. "You see, the tractor tanker was a special lake-stocking vehicle. It was fitted with a huge tank--hundreds of gallons of water, I would guess—that probably contained a couple thousand rainbow trout."

The fish liberator at the wheel of the truck didn't waste any time. He backed down the boat ramp, and used a black six-inch-wide hose to empty his cargo. In about 30 minutes the entire surface of the lake was **flush** with fish.

"It was absolutely spectacular! They were jumping up out of the water and flipping across the surface everywhere. I'd never seen anything quite like it—and Michael just sat there stunned at first," Troy said, slightly breathless at the memory. "He was **ecstatic** watching all of those fish flashing on the water. They were just like the sparkling sunlight coming off the small ripples that you see when a slight breeze is blowing."

He then assured me that I could not imagine how quickly the pair limited out that day. "Michael caught the first one, and then before he was done reeling it in I had a fish on. We actually had to take turns fishing it was so fast and furious! Twelve rainbow trout on two golden treble hooks in less than a half an hour!" he spurted out, boasting that the catch had to be some sort of record.

I was trying to stick with Troy's story, but I was getting a bit frustrated. "OK, Troy cut to the punchline, will you?" I interrupted. "I still don't know how you could possibly have had a bad day while fishing."

A slow smile crept across his face, and he looked at me incredulously. "Eddy, Eddy, Eddy, don't you get it? Ever since the fish-stocking incident, my son has gotten the idea that the fish should just hop into the boat," he said. "After an experience like that, how could I ever get him to understand how to go out and really enjoy the **solitude** of the chase, especially since he's still so young?"

Laughing out loud, I said "Jeese, Troy, I thought I had heard some good fish stories, but that one takes the cake, can I put that one in my book?

Moral of the story: Self-discipline isn't learned in a day.

19
Happy Thanksgiving

For 10 years I had been going home for Christmas on the train. Although it is 10 times more comfortable and faster by a day, to fly home, it usually costs hundreds of dollars less on the train. While chatting with a coworker, John, about the upcoming holiday, he mentioned that he was driving back east for the Thanksgiving holiday. After thinking about it for a while, I suggested he drop me off in Billings at my sister's home. We could make the time go faster together, and he could save some money on gas.

My thinking was that my entire family would go to Grannie Annie's house in Glasgow, Montana, for Thanksgiving. Then I would then be able to take the train back to Portland, Oregon. After a couple of phone calls to our respective families, the road trip was on; this year I would be able to substitute thanksgiving for Christmas. The promise of a less crowded train was very appealing indeed.

John was a very good driver, and since I had taken the route many times before and had a copy of mapquest in my pocket, I was an equally competent navigator. The first 500 miles to my Aunt Rosie and Uncle Ralph's R and R Ranch outside of Missoula was a breeze. It isn't really a ranch, but rather a 25-acre hay farm surrounding a mansion which Uncle Ralph had planned for and built on for years. I admired his sacrificing of vacations, new cars, expensive clothes and spare time while providing for his family. In retrospect, through discipline, he had attained the American dream of owning a small slice of heaven, before retiring on a very modest income from the U.S. Forest Service.

Early the next morning my aunt and uncle's hospitality was **impeccable** as usual. The overwhelming smell, which promised hotcakes, sausages, toast, homemade jelly and my personal favorite, sunny-side-up eggs, began to drift into my room just about the time the alarm clocks went off. At 4 a.m. it was dark, of course, but the magnificent outline of the mountain across the valley was already visible from the breakfast nook. Finishing breakfast and packing our bags, we said our good-byes. As a last reminder, Ralph and Rosie cautioned us that it was 28 degrees out and to beware of black ice on the road.

It didn't take long before we found out what they were

talking about. Every few miles we saw the evidence of skids and severe over-steering left in the ice crystals on the road.

About an hour or two down the road we came to Bozeman, which happens to be the place where I was born. I could go on for hours on how beautiful a spot it is, but if you really want an unbiased view I've heard rumors that the book **Zen** and the Art of Motorcycle Maintenance has a **compelling** description of it. Leaving Bozeman, we started up Lolo pass. It's is a nice climb featuring stunning boulders and **surreal** scenery—like something out of a Beverly Doolittle print. It's too bad we hadn't had time to bring the mountain bikes along.

Besides a quick stop at an out of the way convenience market for some world famous Montana state beef jerky, we arrived in Billings, and John and I parted ways.

Thanksgiving was the normal **mêlée** of what we as a family had been doing for years. The three-wheelers had been replaced with four-wheelers, which was annoying for my nephew Jonathan, who claimed it is more dangerous to ride a four-wheeler on two wheels than a three-wheeler on two wheels. The old snowmobile that I had run into a stream years before had been replaced with a souped-up version that my dad claimed had enough power to go across that stream on top of the water. Too bad I didn't have that back when I was nine, I muttered to myself upon hearing the claim!

Of course, the satisfying gathering it went by too fast as

usual, and I found myself on the same unchanging train platform that I had been on so many times before.

Except for the occasional herd of antelope the train ride through the plains of Montana is rather, well, boring. And that is even assuming that you find funny-looking deer chewing their cuds exciting. However, I've found over the years that this **trek** is an excellent way to catch up on my reading. One other task I accomplish on the long ride is to write down goals, which I substitute for resolutions--as goals can be broken up, to enable achievement versus resolutions which always seem to be broken!

`One stop I always look forward to is the little town of Havre. Normally, the train is scheduled to stop for about 45 minutes to an hour, to let freight trains pass. The reason I liked it, however, was that in addition to stretching my legs I could go and have a quick beer at PJ'S Bar, located just across the street.

This stop in Havre was to be different from all of the beer stops I had previously **partaken** of on my way back from Glasgow to Portland. The overhead speaker instructed that we would only be stopping at Havre for 10 minutes. A few minutes later, I asked a passing conductor about the previous announcement. He replied that two freight trains were running late, and if we didn't start out of Havre early and make it to Shelby about 100 miles up the line and wait there, we would be the ones running three hours late, not the freight trains!

Regardless of the short stop, I was determined to pay a

buck and have a quick fresh glass of draft on tap. Waiting for the train to come to a stop I kidded myself that I was really saving $5 by not purchasing on the train one of those plastic cups of beer, poured out of a can. Racing across the street in a T-shirt, I made the trip across the street as fast my **Nike Air Max** running shoes could carry me. It was definitely winter in Montana, and even though the sun was blasting like a propane torch it was well below freezing outside. Opening the door to PJ's Bar I welcomed the gush of warm air with relief.

Three steps in I realized something was wrong. Although a couple of lights were on, the place was deserted. There were no **patrons**, no card games, and worst of all, no bartenders! I used the restroom, checked the store room, grabbed some free beer nuts and pretzels, called out, "Is anybody here?" and then finally decided to exit. Even though I was **tempted** to pour myself a cold one I resisted the urge and made my way back to the train.

Still puzzled, I acknowledged that I normally made this trip on or around the Christmas holiday, and that maybe the bar hadn't even been open. Or perhaps someone had forgotten to lock up. Despite my disappointing fiasco I was back on the tracks minutes later reading a good book, which oddly enough contained a passage referring to the Ten Commandments.

The next stop was Shelby. We were informed that the stop would be well over an hour, but that the train would leave **precisely** on its normally scheduled time. I set the alarm feature on my watch, and asked the conductor how we made up so much time. His reply was that the engineer had kicked up the train's speed to 75 miles an hour to keep on our schedule, as freight trains take **precedence** over passenger trains.

I decided to go out for a walk in the booming city of Shelby, only with a coat this time! **Donning** my boots and some gloves I set out across multiple sets of tracks and made my way to a street sign that read Main Street. Looking up the street a distance I saw a neon bar sign brightly proclaiming simply "Oasis." I walked up, stopped, and thought, what the heck I've got over an hour. I waltzed inside.

Before the door had shut the owner immediately introduced himself as Tom and in the classic bartender style asked, "What'll it be?" While handing me a cold draft before I even sat down, he asked if I was new to town (probably anticipating the prospect of gaining a new regular, I thought). I replied that the train was being delayed due to late-running freight trains coming from the west. With that, he raised his voice a little so that the 20 or so people in the bar could hear his response, "Well, why didn't you bring them all with you? We're a friendly bunch here!"

And indeed they were. As soon as I finished my beer someone else would buy me another before I had even finished the one I was drinking. At the time, I didn't mind, after all, I had started telling my best fishing stories and everyone seemed to be smiling and laughing at them. However, after about five free beers, the theme from the movie "Deliverance" started playing in the back of my mind. Just as another round was coming up, the alarm on my watch went off. I quickly finished my punchline, gulped down the entire contents of the glass as fast as I could, excused myself and thanked everyone for the hospitality. Then I made for the door at lightning speed.

Trudging through the evidence of early winter, mixed with a dusky **smattering** of snow that was coming in from the east, I started the quarter mile **jaunt** to the train diagonally across what appeared to be a vacant field. I did this in an attempt to save some time, instead of going down the street and up to the station in an L shaped route that most rational people would do.

About halfway to the train I heard a thunderous **salvo** piercing the silence from behind me. Run--the train is leaving! Of course I looked back, and saw that the entire group from the bar was standing on the sidewalk. Those turkeys were trying to make me miss my train! I kicked up my heels and pumped my hands while standing still and got a huge laugh. Best of all, I had a belly full of free beer to sustain me!

Moral of the story: Beware of seemingly free gifts from strangers! Or, if you ever find yourself in Shelby, Montana, stop by the Oasis and tell the barkeep that you're from the train!

20
Horseshoe Hill

Horseshoe Hill is the **conjoining** curve that links two separate avenues that connect to the main drag on the upper side of Bellevue, a mid-sized city just east of Seattle, Washington. The infamous hill is really just the nickname of the impossibly steep U part that connects each street, as one of the two thoroughfares is roughly 60 feet higher than the other.

In the summertime, which lasts just a couple of months, Belleview really lives up to its French name Beautiful view. Anywhere you look there are magnificent views of Lake Washington, tall trees, flowers, and abundant Parks. During the other 9 temperate months it is generally wet and the perfect vision of, well, grey. On rare occasions however, it can be snow white, and bring all car traffic on Horseshoe hill to a standstill. This by the way is great if you are a kid!

When we went to the hill during those rare snow days, I always brought my Flexible Flyer, which was far and away the fastest sled on the hill. There wasn't anything visibly different about my sled, compared to anyone else's on that hill; mine was superior because of the fact that it was waxed and tuned by the best ex-ski instructor in the world: my dad. It also didn't hurt that only-die hard seasoned sledders (like yours truly) would start off running with the sled in hand, jump on in mid flight, and land with a bone-bruising jar, to get a serious speed jumpstart. The crowning advantage, at the time, was that I happened to be the fastest runner in first grade.

The good thing about Horseshoe Hill was that there was a **spur** trail at the bottom, which led to Eastgate Elementary School. Though it wasn't very steep, the spur trail had just enough altitude to enable sledders starting off at the top of the hill to go nearly a quarter of a mile without stopping. When it snowed, kids circled in an endless loop, from the top of the spur trail to the bottom and back up again. From above, the line of children would have looked much like a bent **infinity** shape, as the corner to the spur trail was a tight hard angle.

This corner was nicknamed Chicken Point, and it was the scene of many a wipeout throughout the winter. Speed demons trying to beat their own records usually ended up in the laurel hedge. Occasionally, collisions between sledders and unsuspecting pedestrians occurred; but for the most part, after a couple of crashes most kids learned their limitations. It had only taken me 118 crashes to get the picture.

One Saturday in January, after my morning breakfast routine—it consisted of pancakes and my mom's homemade artificial maple syrup--the hill beckoned. Well, not exactly, but when I saw my friend Andy and his mean big brother, Marshal, taking off with their sleds, it seemed to me that the hill was calling

I hurried as fast as my legs could carry me, pulling my sled behind me. It was soon clear, though, that I wouldn't be catching up with Andy and Marshal. When I arrived at the top of the hill, they were nowhere to be seen. Where did they go? That soon became my $64 question. If they had climbed to the top, I reasoned, the boys would have gone whizzing by me just about the time I reached Chicken Point. Something was up, and I was determined to find out what it was.

Taking a flying leap, the Flexible Flyer earned its keep. Dragging my right foot skillfully and leaning on one rail to make the corner, I careened into a slide that would have impressed an Indy 500 race-car driver. Those guys wouldn't get away from Eddy this time! I muttered to myself.

To my utter surprise, the boys weren't at the bottom of the hill either.

Giving up and dragging my sled up the path, the sight of my neighbors startled me. The reason that I hadn't been able to spot them was because they were building a jump on the steep side of the gradual path leading to the school. From the point of my eye level, the boys had been **obscured** from sight. I looked at the side hill, which was angled at about 45 degrees, and my eyes lit up. "Can I help?" I blurted excitedly. "Only if you can sled down the steep part and not wreck," Marshal replied sternly. Pointing my sled down the embankment and envisioning the ride, the rush was simultaneously thrilling and scary.

Within minutes, all three of us were bringing snow over. The pile of snow left over from the schools recently plowed parking lot would make a huge jump. We were transporting it heap by heap on a lid of a school trash can. Ever **emulating** our fathers, we pretended that we were going to be future Boeing Engineers. This of course was evidenced by the fact that we had placed this round tin contraption squarely on top of Andy's flexible flyer, and it worked!

Our monster mound was fast approaching four feet in height when we heard my friends' father bellowing from behind us, "Andy, Marshal! You two didn't get permission to go sledding--you're both grounded. Come up here now!" They knew they were both in big trouble, so they left immediately without the whining that first- and second-graders are typically known for.

Laughing to myself, I thought, "Wow! I'll have this jump all to myself!" As I climbed to the top of Horseshoe

Hill, the urge to fly was making my heart pound as much as the effort of the ascent itself. I stood at the top, knowing somehow that my best run ever was about to happen. I zoomed down like an Olympian on a professional **luge.**

Rounding the first corner in style, using my right foot drag trick as a **rudder**, I started on the second leg of my journey. Slowing slightly to make the 90-degree turn down the steep slope, my target was in sight and I was in perfect alignment. "Three, Two, One," I counted, and squinted my eyes in anticipation. But I went nowhere; I became wedged into that jump. We boys had not realized that we'd have had to pack the snow a whole lot harder to make a good jump. So instead of taking off like lightning, my sled's rails had sunk straight into our mound, stopping me dead in my tracks.

At first I was really upset by what had happened, especially so because the force of the sudden stop sent bursts of pain shooting in to my wrists. Peering over my steering bars, I started to feel a bit of relief when I considered what might have transpired if my attempt had not failed. Peering over the four-foot mound, it occurred to me that my landing from the jump would have been 10 times more painful than my unexpected stop.

Moral of the story: Be thankful for dumb luck when it happens.

21

Ice Cave In

My first season working at Mount Rainier started with the mandatory park safety meeting for all new hires. Aside from the usual two reminders--don't feed the rats in cute fur coats and sign in at all trailheads—the ranger spouted out a new rule that I hadn't heard of: Don't go into the ice caves. Looking back, I suppose that global warming had started in the early 1990's.

Then we new hires were treated to a short film on park safety that concerned park rangers had put together. I'm not sure why anyone would tell people not to go in to an ice cave and then immediately show riveting footage of the incredible danger zones. The **ethereal** images, of the semi-**translucent** ceilings and blue **opaque** walls, proved too much of a temptation for a couple of the wayward hikers in attendance. After all, the picture depicted ice chunks the size of baseballs, which surely would hurt if they hit you. We figured out that, statistically anyway, the odds of being in the cave when one of those nuggets came down would only be about one in 10,000.

It did take about a month before Tom and I were able to find out a location of an ice cave that was near enough to our quarters to manage visiting in a single day. The park personnel had been collectively and successfully tight-lipped about the ice cave locations, for a reason we later learned: The year before someone visiting a staffer had died in one from a blow to the head from a basketball-sized chunk of ice, and the aftermath was pretty devastating to the rescue party.

Since Tom and I both had cars we devised a hiking route that would afford an uphill climb from one of the washed-out road trails on the west side of the mountain and leave us with an easy downhill trek to the lodge. Then we would pick up the car where we had left it that night or the next morning. We mapped out precisely our eight-mile route, and as we knew from experience that one mile trekking through woods can easily equal six miles in walking time. As a precaution, we also took two days' **rations** along with us.

The trek along the major road that had been washed out was mostly trouble-free. The only washed-out section had in actuality been the very beginning, so we made good time. The climb up the rock-strewn stream also proved unproblematic; in **verity**, it was merely a hike up a threemile uneven set of stairs--with an occasional branch for a handrail.

We reached the glacier just before 10 a.m., two hours ahead of schedule. We had covered five miles in five hours. Checking our map and coordinates to soothe our **qualms**, we discovered that we were indeed on track. The next part of our heroes' journey was a half mile trek across the glacier to the cave whose location we had identified through intellectual **nefarious sleuthing**.

Since we had extra time on our hands, Tom and I mutually decided to follow the base of the ice sheet instead of going across the face; having traversed many glaciers we knew that one crevasse would end our endeavor.

Fortunately, we had again made the right decision and we made better time than expected. We were able to find the approximate end of the cave entrance by discovering evidence of a slightly used trail of sorts that led up the glacier. Getting cocky now, given our smooth expedition to date, we patted ourselves on the back and laughed at how easy this adventure had been.

The entrance to the cave was smaller than we had thought it would be, but we went in without **trepidation**. What we saw was awe-inspiring. The film hadn't begun to do this cave justice. The icy **cobalt** walls didn't seem cold and lifeless, they actually seemed more like mermaids calling out to us and inviting our warm touch. The blue color was as warm and enticing as Crater Lake's icy depths, and the freezing caress upon our exposed flesh was intensely refreshing. Our **euphoria**, however, was checked, at about 25 feet into our newfound fantasyland, when disaster nearly struck. A chunk of ice about the size of my buddy's Lincoln Continental fell from the ceiling a mere 50 feet away from us!

Slowly and gently backing out of the cave, we looked at each other, and I whispered, "Gee, Tom, what were they saying about not going into the ice caves?" Peering out from the entrance we decided to try to get back to the lodge in time for dinner.

We had two options: to go back the way we came, or try the route we had penned out on paper and left in the glove compartment of my car. Since we were now three hours ahead of schedule, we decided that we would stick to the original plan. Hiking down and around to the original stream we had come up, we made our way down the 800-foot drop.

Slowly we traversed down the western side of the canyon. Fortunately there were many handholds, easy to navigate staircase like **serrations**, and a declining grade of about 30 percent down to the creek bottom. It wasn't quite technical climbing, but it was slick and dark and wet at times.

Going up the other side wasn't that difficult either; we didn't need ropes or our ice axes, as the terrain was all dry rock. The 1,600 feet had taken us two hours, and the remainder of the trip home was an even path we had both traversed many times. The only obstacle now was an ice sheet roughly 200 yards wide and 200 yards long.

It was about 4 p.m. when we approached the final leg. Acting on the understanding that all individuals have free will, Tom and I had long before decided that if one of us wanted to go one way, the other one didn't have to take the same route if another preferred path was nearby. I chose to be safe and go up the muddy side of this small glacier. Using the sheet of ice on one side as a solid anchor and rock and dirt on the other, I had a solid channel to make the climb up safely.

My buddy decided to go straight up the face. We both were making about the same time, but I resembled more like the innards of a clam than a man as I was sandwiched between the mountain and the small glacier. Looking over, I saw Tom's right foot dislodge a massive chunk of ice, one that likely weighed at least 100 pounds. Its downward slide covered the 100 yards in a few seconds and went hurtling over the embankment to a silent end. Tom, however, was moving much more slowly. Watching the sheet of ice flying off an 800-foot cliff must have terrified Tom, who was now hurtling down this sheet of ice headfirst. Knowing that he was moving about as fast as a skier, I knew that I couldn't do anything but watch in dismay and disbelief.

At that point in time I wasn't worried about Tom dying. Somewhere in my mind, I had already declared him dead, seconds after I witnessed the streak of blood trailing down the ice sheet. The thing I was worried about was what I was going to say to Tom's father, who was the type of guy who had achieved 16 letters in high school and who could still whoop the living daylights out of both of us at the same time.

Miraculously, Tom stopped short of going off the embankment by a matter of mere inches, by his own account later. He shuddered when he reported that he had, quite simply, "stared straight down into the depths of hell." He recounted that had been aiming for the only solidly anchored rock on the lip of the edge of the cliff by using his right forearm as a rudder.

Bellowing out a shout of relief, Tom demonstrated that stubborn is as stubborn does; he had to prove to himself that he could make it up the ice sheet where he had failed before. Of course, I was on edge myself while he made his second attempt, but this time, to my relief, he made it without any more bloodshed.

Moral of the story: When the best-made plans go wrong, maintain your faculties.

22

In A Ditch With Rich

I first got to know Rich while attending my first Self Contained Underwater Breathing Apparatus (Scuba) class at Southern Oregon State University. It's funny how you can live in the same apartment complex and not really get to know someone even though the person lives barely 50 feet away. It turned out that both Rich and I had wanted to get Scuba certified for a long time, but we hadn't wanted the added tuition expense coming out of our own pockets while simultaneously paying for the **prolific** amount of gear required.

Inadvertently, we were paired up in the class and it turned out that we had much more in common than just scuba, and thrift. Because we lived so near each other, the ease of hooking up for runs, bike rides, and other extracurricular activities, naturally induced us to become good friends. Heck, I even got him a job as a delivery driver at Pizza Shack.

Another benefit of our neighborly proximity was that, with our class being held at 7 a.m. sharp five days a week, our other buddy system, using two alarm clocks, proved an indispensable arrangement by the end of the first week of class. Guess who bought the coffee if we weren't out the door by 6:30 a.m. and the other one had to knock?

By the end of the quarter we were ready to go down to Catalina Island, off the coast of Southern California, for our certification dives. As luck would have it, our instructors were flying down and needed someone to take their gear. When Rich brought this to my attention, I thought about it, and said, "Well, how much are they offering?" "All of the gas money, round trip," Rich replied.

"So, that would mean you're getting a free trip, right?" I said, sarcastically, but in a joking manner. His view was that he was entitled to a finder's fee. "Sure," I said. "But what about the wear and tear on the tires, the oil and filter cost of a 2,000-mile trip? And that's not to mention the insurance, depreciation on the car, and the fact that I'm responsible if any of the stuff gets stolen or my car breaks down."

He shrugged his shoulders, looked at me squarely, and said, "Eddy, we'll figure out something."

Eddy Ivy

We were able to complete our finals a day ahead of time to head south, so we decided to start off very early in the morning so that we could take in a baseball game at Dodger Stadium when we got to Los Angeles. The plan was to switch drivers back and forth, drive as long as we could manage to stay awake, and then find a place to sleep somewhere.

Managing to get over the Siskiyou Pass and into California before five a.m. gave us a definite feeling of accomplishment. An hour or so later, just south of Mount Shasta, I saw a small green piece of paper fly across the road. Bizarre though it may sound, in my mind's eye it looked, unmistakably to me, like a Federal Reserve note. I couldn't resist my curiosity.

Stopping in the middle of nowhere was something I don't normally do, so Rich understandably asked, "What's up, Eddy?" I told him that I thought I saw a green bill fly across the road. I shut off the engine I asked him to help me look for the paper.

Sure enough, it was a $20. I'm sure Rich wouldn't have believed it if he hadn't been the one to find it. Dinner wouldn't be raw oatmeal, after all! Since I always stop for gas as soon as the needle hits the half-way mark, we decided to stop at the next mini-mart we could find instead of stopping at a regular gas station. Grabbing a couple of Big Gulps and a few "half off" dry burger specials, we were ready to go again. Checking our new found resources Rich exclaimed that we had $16 left for a nice dinner somewhere down the line, to boot!

After we had gassed up in more ways than one, we hit the road again. In what seemed like a flash I found it was getting dark. I asked Rich if he would clean off my glasses, which had picked up some Pepsi fizz on their lenses that was starting to **irritate** me and cloud my vision. "Sure," he said, while I handed him my frames.

As he **meticulously** cleaned the glasses with one of those paper handy wipes that contain **isopropyl** alcohol, he ventured: "Eddy, um. How well can you see without these?"

I assured Rich that I could make out the fuzzy car in front of us and the lines on the sides of the road. "No, I'm serious, Eddy," he said. "Tell me, what does that sign say?" What sign?" I replied casually. I had my glasses back in a jiffy.

It turned out that it that the main reason my eyes were getting blurry was that it was past 3 a.m.; we were both just plain tired. As we had no interest in camping right next to Interstate 5, we took the first exit that offered an official on-and-off ramp.

Proceeding down the paved road one mile, we found a small road and drove about a quarter mile or so until, finally, we came to a minor pull-off area alongside the tiny one-lane dirt road. Scouting the area with our Halogen underwater Scuba flashlights we felt comfortable that we had adequate protection from any unlikely morning traffic.

To be on the safe side, I parked my car at a 45-degree

angle in this pullout, which would alert anyone driving this little used road to our presence. We proceeded to unroll our sleeping bags in the adjoining dry and, to us at the time, seemingly cozy ditch. Even though we had nice air mattresses and full scuba tanks with which we could have filled them with ease, we were too tired to bother.

I remember the sunshine hitting my face at dawn and then rolling over to hide from the light. I wasn't quite ready to wake up, and besides, I wanted to let Rich be the one to make the managerial decision about when to get going. Then, suddenly, from out of nowhere, it seemed, a semi-trailer came roaring by, spreading a fine powdery dust in its wake and rattling us mightily. Looking up at Rich, we said in **unison**, as if we'd rehearsed our lines, "It's time to go."

When we stood up we realized that we were a mere 75 yards from someone's front yard! To make matters more uncomfortable, we saw that a family of four was having breakfast out on their front porch. I would have given the $4 we still had left over from dinner to know what was going through their minds when we both stood up, next to the white station wagon parked out in the middle of nowhere. Hopping into our getaway vehicle, we laughed and zipped back on to the highway. After all, we had a ballgame to get to!

Moral of the story: If you're tired, find a safe place to pull over and take a nap.

23
Instant Replay

My parents were fairly **liberal** people, so they left it pretty much up to me to decide how to pursue my college education and what I wanted to do with my life. Since I had my own money, a few miscellaneous tuition scholarships, and a real love of skiing I decided to take a term off of college and do nothing but ski. My parents weren't overjoyed, but they had learned firsthand that I was pretty good at taking care of myself.

By the end of my senior high school year I had saved up an extra large chunk of change. This fact was enough to assure them that I wasn't going to be whining about money anytime soon. Packing up my stuff, I left and headed off to a stay with a high school buddy, Russ. Fortunately, we had stayed in contact and I was able to **cajole** him into allowing me to stay a couple of nights with him in Bend, Oregon until I could find an apartment.

My *modus operandi* made Scrooge look like a **spendthrift**, so my decision to move into a spare room in a house with a bunch of ski fanatics, rather than finding my own place, didn't surprise my folks. I soon learned that my new roommates all worked part time at Oregon's Mount Bachelor in the winter and full time in the summer for the U.S. Forest Service. At first I felt a little like an outsider, as the seven other coinhabitants--two guys, three gals and an older married couple—had known one another for many years. But even with that crowd, the huge house had room for one more.

My original plan was to only pay for a $225 midweek pass, and only ski Monday through Friday. With a little input from my newfound friends, I had come up with a new plan. Buy the Midweek Pass, and then for a $2 single-ride pass so I could take the highest running chair-lift on the weekends. At the top I would offer to carry people's skis up to the summit of Mount Bachelor for $10.

My business idea was a major hit. It was easy for me to run up with two pair of skis, and come down and do it again, in less than a half an hour. Many times, I would be passing the first "customer" with the second one's skis before the first person even got to their skis.

This worked well. Not only was I able to buy a full-day pass, but I could also afford to pick up the tab for two happy-hour specials at the lodge. Those juicy burger baskets included a stein of beer and steak fries. I innocently established this evening routine with the cute part-time chairlift attendant, Kathy--one of my roommates, who was soon to become my full-time girlfriend. On those days when the weather was not so hot for skiing and too foggy for me to go to the top, I was stuck buying a couple of one-time passes, just so I could get in a couple of runs with Kathy on her breaks.

On one day when the weather was especially **bleak**, I encountered friends from the Fox Rim Lodges and the married couple from my house. They were practicing back flips under the red chair line lift, and all of them readily classified as ski bums. In fact, they hadn't even bothered to pay for a ticket. That was not because they didn't have the money, but rather because they had hauled up by backpack four cases of dirt-cheap generic Beer Beer, which wasn't allowed on the lift, I'm told. Looking at the label I was surprised to see that it was brewed in Olympia, Washington. "Gee," I said, loudly. "Olympia! I wonder who really brews this stuff." When my friends smirked, I decided that the joke was on me.

It takes a little courage to try your first backflip on snow skis. Since I knew what to expect from years of spectacular wipeouts, I also knew that a little alcohol beforehand would help to deaden the pain of what I was surely soon to experience. Watching the action while drinking one of my buddy's brews, my taste buds came alive. "What *is* this stuff?" I asked, savoring a sip. "We brew our own, Babe, and it's even cheaper than the Beer Beer," Jody the married petite blonde, laughingly offered by way of mischievous explanation. "And we're all big recyclers, Eddy."

Pretty groovy, I thought, taking the ale tale even more seriously than before.

Sitting there listening to the rotating audience's cheers when a good flip was landed, **interspersed** with their howls of sympathetic pain, the urge to attempt the act was too strong to overcome.

About two dozen attempts into my new act, I had mastered the nerve-wracking back flip. I had endured the red chair lift's audience for an hour and was starting to come out on top more often than not. It wasn't that I was perfect at the flips, but the fact that it was a terrific powder day essentially removed my fear of wiping out. Soon, even after imbibing a few of the seven-percent drinks, my success ratio was at least as high as my buddies' was.

Unfortunately, I wanted to do a perfect one, and so did all the rest of my colleagues. We were bound and determined to catch a great piece of air and land perfectly, as we were all rating each other. Besides, we still had two cases of home-brewed goodness to last the entire afternoon--and nobody wanted to have to haul a full case down the hill. Finally, it was only 1 o'clock, and even though the lifts closed at 3:30 p.m., we weren't using them.

Kathy **sauntered** over, skidding to a stop and spraying us all with snow. Then she showed us all up. She was 30, and from all appearances, was headed for the Lift

Operator/Park Ranger lifetime program. Unflinching and without warning, she headed for our ramp. Boom! She landed a perfect backflip in style, full of grace and with her long black hair flying. Handing her a beer after she hiked up the 20 yards from the jump, I looked at her with utter admiration, and said, "Here goes 87."

I took off and would have scored a two, per our simple rating system, except that my ski hat fell off, which relegated me to a one. After I crawled back up and sat down, awaiting my next turn, Kathy looked at me, and laughed. "And just how long are you going to keep this up, Eddy?" she inquired, a slight annoyance creeping in to her tone.

"Until I hit a perfect one or we run out of beer," I replied. After that, 88, 89, 94, 101 and 116 all were near perfect, and even though we were running low on light, beer and energy, I **persevered**. Number 126 changed everything. I don't know why or how, but right after I landed, someone from the chairlift yelled out, "Wow, that was perfect, man!"

Whatever it was, that backflip was good enough for me, and I was free to go home satisfied that I had fulfilled my pledge.

The next morning I woke up and hauled my sorry butt down the stairs to the kitchen. Kathy's room was just adjacent to the kitchen, and she was already up making coffee for everyone. "You look like hell, Eddy," she said with a laugh. "What's the matter? Too much of that improved Beer Beer?"

"No, Kathy," I replied **gingerly**. "Just too many 1's and 2's."

Moral of the story: Perfection always has a price.

24

Jupiter Rising

Two years after finishing graduate school, to find myself working for a Fortune 500 company—which is what I went to college for—found me in the middle of the stench of civilization in Portland, Oregon. The money was good, but it was darn near impossible to find time for my cherished sprees in the trees and other adventures. And even if I could get away, finding a buddy to go along was becoming more challenging, as an ever-increasing number of my friends were getting married and having children.

One afternoon in late June, while chatting with a still single buddy from school who had made his home in Sacramento, California, I discovered that Darren had scheduled the same week of vacation that I had, the last week of August. Upon this stroke of fate, we decided to hook up at his house and explore Yosemite for a week.

Six weeks later, I was on the road. My trip down south would take an entire day, and long before the time I had made the California border Sammy Haggar's song "I Can't Drive 55" was getting old. In fact, after going up the Siskiyou Pass at 55 and being passed by a semi-truck, of all things, I decided I was driving too slowly. Setting the cruise control for exactly 62 miles per hour to avoid a speeding ticket, I quietly thanked God for inventing cruise control.

Arriving at his house just before suppertime, we did what any two red-blooded American boys would do. Yes, we ordered pizza! Later after finishing the large pepperoni pizza we found that Darren's 100-quart cooler wouldn't fit in the back of my car without removing the back seat. After navigating that albeit minor **ordeal**, I was ready for some much-needed and well-deserved sleep. After all, we wanted to go around to the back side of Yosemite to camp and then go see the famous Bristlecone pines.

It was a good thing we were going around to the back side of the park. As it turned out, the west entrance of Yosemite had a lot of roadwork going on and there was a traffic jam in the middle of nowhere. We just smiled and kept on driving around the park's **perimeter**. The interest in this part of our **jaunt** was derived from the fact that the forest was home to a tree whose core dated to 4,767 years old and was aptly named Methuselah.

Driving on we were understandably puzzled when we found ourselves facing a sign that read: Elevation 7,000 feet. Over and over we saw the sign, on every little hill we traversed, to the point that we started to think we had been sucked in to a twisted Twilight Zone-type rerun. Whether it was a planned placement based on actual fact, or merely some bored park director's idea of a sick joke, we wondered nonetheless why there weren't any other elevation-marker signs for lower or higher spots. Perhaps, Darren joked, there had been a surplus "Blue Light Special" from the Department of Transportation, whose fun-loving staff knew that we just wanted one sign telling us that the elevation had dropped to 6,999 feet!

Finally, we found the road that led to the **Bristlecone pine** forest, the infamous Ancient Bristlecone Scenic Byway. It is a winding, steep two-lane road with an incline average of a five- to six-percent grade. In an effort to keep my four-cylinder car engine cool enough to handle the stress, we kept the heater going with the windows wide open—a little-known way of keeping the temperature gauge at an acceptable range. This trick works especially well in the mountains, and I have yet to be the one of those guys parked along the side the road with steam spouting out of the car's engine.

We stopped for lunch at a pullout on the west side of the winding road, which had a picnic table facing Yosemite. After eating a couple of sandwiches we took a dozen **panoramic** shots of the stunning Sierra Nevada mountain range. The nature of which, at the time, like a still photo of the famous Western photographer Ansel

Adams, only in color. Trying to capture as much of the 350-mile long range as we could, we took multiple shots side by side to later tape together later as a memento of this 100 degree plus scorching-hot side trip. A half an hour later we were back in the car, approaching the entrance of a desolated parking lot, where a small trailer sported a couple of lime-green Forest Service vehicles.

Walking the short loop of the upper trail we tried to make out the **Alpha** and **Omega** and **Methuselah** trees, to which we had obtained top-secret access from old documents, as the trees identities are now secret to protect them. We spotted the Alpha tree based on the photocopy we made of a photo in a 1960s-era dictionary, but we were unable to guess which one was the Omega or the Methuselah.

Darren and I then launched into an argument over whether the drilled core holes should have been filled in to prevent insect damage. To settle the matter, we decided to go back to the ranger station and ask the green uniformed professionals. On opening the door and walking in, standing behind the desk was the most gorgeous green-skinned blonde creature I had ever seen in my life. Trying not to be a flirt, I attempted to collect myself as I posed my question about the dating holes not being filled in around the park trail. She responded with a brilliant smile that nearly rivaled one a Miss America pageant winner might emit as the tiara is being laid on her shining locks. "I would be glad to answer that question, just as soon as you sign the guest book in the corner," she said, pointing to the counter.

When I looked at the book I saw that it was empty I deduced that Darren and I had been the only park visitors that day. Back at the desk I told the woman that I signed in my buddy as well, and said, "Now, what is the answer to our question? After all, we've got a bet going here."

Smiling broadly again, she explained, "Well, I was told by the higher ups that it attracts the endangered white-fanged mosquitoes."

Laughing at her unexpected response, I replied, "Gee, thanks. That sure helps—and, by the way, that is a really beautiful ring you're wearing." She thanked me and smiled again, and said, joking, "Yes, my husband says that the ring helps to keep the white-fanged mosquitoes away!"

Annoyed at the attention I was receiving and by the beating I was taking, my buddy chirped in, and said, "Well, ma'am, you had better tell your husband to get you a bigger ring soon because that one doesn't seem to be working very well any more!"

"I'll be sure to tell him that you guys weren't impressed," she **quipped**, attempting to end the exchange.

As we walked out the door, Darren said, "Eddy, I hope you didn't put your license plate number on that register. "Well, I hate to tell you this, Darren," I said, "but if Mickey Mouse and Donald Duck from Anaheim show up dead in the Pacific, it'll be entirely your fault!"

Chortling, we hopped in the car and were on our way

down the snaking road to the next stop on our agenda: Yosemite National Park.

On the way down we discussed the possibility that the pretty ranger might not actually be married. I held the belief that the 1-carat ring was actually a **cubic zirconium**, while my buddy insisted it was a real diamond. Darren thought that she was married; I suspected she wasn't. Not able to prove either point, we kept this conversation up all the way down the hill, yet we still couldn't come up with an acceptable **parameter** for a bet.

When we finally made it to the official park entrance shack to pay the $5 fee we both did a double-take and looked at each other, bewildered, as we eyed the woman in the booth. Forking over the Abe Lincoln-emblazoned bill, I said, "You're not going to believe this, but you have a double." She replied, "Hey, that's the oldest line in the book, buddy, so I hope that's not your best one!"

"No, really," I replied. "You wouldn't believe it. We just came from the Bristlecone pine forest, and there is a blonde ranger there wearing a fake 1-carat diamond who claims she's married to a forester."

At that, she started laughing so hard she almost fell off her seat. After she sighed in relief, she admitted the truth. "Cindy is my identical twin sister, and the ring is a fake! But she is married, only not to a ranger."

Now it was our turn to laugh. We turned to each other and cried out, simultaneously, "You owe me 50 bucks!"

146

Fortunately, we had arrived late enough in the day that no other cars were behind us, which gave us ample time to chat with the "double," whose name was Candy.

She had noticed that my car had a couple of national park stickers on the window and asked about them. Replying that we had both worked in both Crater Lake and Mount Rainier, she smiled and asked if we wanted to go on a ranger-guided day hike for park employees the following day, given that we were sort of park employees. "Sure," I said, after Darren nodded his approval. "So long as it's not your sister's husband in command," we replied, after detailing our name switching prank to her.

After ensuring we had the place and time details straight for the next day's hike, we asked why there had been so many cars at the west end of the park. She told us that hundreds of people had come out to be away from the lights of the city so that they might better witness the meteors that were supposed to be slamming into Jupiter that very evening. With this piece of information, we knew we wouldn't be spending that night in the already full campgrounds.

The parking lots were also full and overcrowded, and we were told that the rangers wouldn't be writing any tickets that night. There were so many people gathering around telescopes that they had given up on enforcing the rules and punishing any usual **infractions** for the evening. It was kind of a letdown for us, however; we had wanted to get away from the crowds, but instead found an ant colony of people in every nook and cranny of Yosemite!

After we had gotten our fill of free entertainment by going from 60-power telescopes to bigger ones the size of cannons, we decided to go set up my Old Blue tent. Adhering to Yosemite's park guidelines of being a mile away from the road, we followed a trail in the bright moonlight and found a nice area to camp. The slightly inclined sparsely treed area was ideal and when we were far enough from the main trail to be "legal" with respect to the park regulations, we were pleasantly surprised that we could still hear the stream.

In a few minutes, we had the tent up and our bags unrolled. Darren took off for the stream. "What are you doing" I asked. He said, "Eddy, you're not going to believe this, but when I was a kid my parents took me here--and I just remembered that there is a pool over in these falls that feels just like a Jacuzzi!"

"You first," I said, thinking he was joking.

It turned out that he wasn't kidding. The intense heat of the day had made the stream warm enough to wade through, and the pool he talked about was indeed a bubbling, churning natural bath. Enjoying the much-needed odor-eating natural Jacuzzi and probable Native American-approved soaking spot was a relief. After all, we would be hiking with a group of other clean and **civilized** people in the morning.

The next morning we were introduced to the group as Mickey and Donald from Crater Lake by our cute blonde friends. We found that we were going on the hike that would end at the top of a ledge that had historically been a fire waterfall. Taking the ranger aside, I asked where his gun was. He looked at me quizzically, and said, "Well, I normally don't take my gun out when on these types of tours, as it looks kind of **intimidating**." I noted that the rangers at Crater Lake had always taken their guns on this type of outing, justifying the practice because of the food that was invariably brought along. "You're right," he said. He returned in a few minutes later with his piece and then we were off.

Of course, when one is prepared, it seems that emergencies don't come up. This hike was no exception. One of the stops was the top of a ledge that had been used decades earlier as a tourist attraction. It seems that rangers would burn up red fir bark in the evening and push the coals over the edge, in the dark of night, to entertain visitors. This event formerly known as the Yosemite Firefall was stopped in 1968 due to environmental concerns. We didn't notice any blatantly visible damage, and in fact dismissed the factoid and enjoyed the fabulous views of the valley. Enjoying the company of these two gorgeous blondes and their gracious attention ended too soon, of course. But we will always be grateful for their hospitality.

Moral of the story: There are too many blondes and hot tubs in California.

P.S. Please send them to Oregon!

25

Laos Hallway

Most people have heard that age-old saying "one man's trash is another man's treasure." That came to mind one afternoon in Portland, Oregon, when I stopped at a well-advertised garage sale, and the prospect of finding anything interesting enough to purchase was **waning** quickly. Turning around and walking out past the piles of trash, the idea of adding a "b" smack dab in the middle of all of the garage sale signs flashed through my mind.

Three steps away from the door, a child's shoe box caught my eye. On a small Post-it note I read the hastily scribbled words: Old topographical maps--10 cents each. Picking up the box and inspecting the table of contents on the inside of the inner box top, I deduced that the maps' owner must have been a real hiking enthusiast back in the 1950's. When an elderly gentleman with a German accent walked up and said, "One dollar and it's yours, young man," I quickly responded with my counter-offer. "How about **six bits**?" I posed. "Sold to the redhead for three quarters," the man boomed, smiling and pretending to tap a hammer to the table.

I decided to pursue the maps' history. "Have you got any advice or words of wisdom for a guy who wants to do hikes in the wilderness?" I asked the seller, a white-haired gentleman who wielded an **authentic** German **Volksmarch** walking stick adorned with several medals representing his various completed hikes. "Well, my best friend was always a **.38 special**," he replied, which suggested to me that he had been a police officer of some capacity in his lifetime.

Testing his **resolve** and curious about his practice of carrying a firearm in the woods, I made my **inquisition**. "Was it worth the extra weight to tow around?" I ventured, which produced a candid reply. "The only critters I've had trouble with in 30 years are the two-legged kind, so here is a question for you: What is your life worth?"

From that point on, my perspective on the safety of the woods changed. I realized that the old man's words were true, and today I always carry a handgun in the wilderness. I am convinced that once you are outside the city limits it is your duty to yourself to take responsibility for your own well-being. I am thankful to our founding fathers that we all still have this choice.

Later that day, going through my newfound treasure, I saw that one of the day hikes listed as No. 11 in the box top was Laos Hallway. This Northwest hike was one of those trails that had been abandoned by the Forest Service for lack of funding and because of notoriously treacherous terrain. After checking my topographical map from 1979, the realization that the hike wasn't listed suggested, to me, anyway, that the box just might be a goldmine of information.

The writing on the aged yellowed map corresponding to his Map # 11 stated the following: Go three quarters of a mile from the snake and follow a small stream deep into the secret **pumice** valley.

After showing a good friend, Tom, my discovery, the two of us decided to make the trip to what we suspected would be our new find. When we arrived at the place where we were instructed to start out, we quickly realized that the promised pull-out on the road didn't exist—at least not for roughly one mile in either direction. That was a little **disconcerting**.

Our first reaction was to suspect that we were onto a secret of sorts, or at least something that was being hidden from the general public. But were we? After parking the truck a mile down the road, we disabling the electrical system as a precaution against theft. Then we hiked to the stream and started down the sides, following the shallow brook.

About a quarter of a mile into our hike, my buddy started to fidget. After I somewhat sarcastically asked, "What's wrong, Tom? You're throwing off **paranoid** vibes," he started shuffling and looking around nervously.

"I, um, don't really know, Eddy," he stammered, "but something is wrong."

I took him seriously, and offered: "Well, chamber up your **Luger** if you want, Tom. We're not in the truck anymore." I scanned the sparsely treed area and was satisfied, for the moment, that we were in no imminent danger from anything or anyone.

Following his lead, I chambered a round and set my safety. Two minutes later, the sides of our brook began to steepen **precipitously**. At about a mile into the hike, it became necessary to descend into the stream-carved valley. The forest had abruptly stopped and gave way to a flat, gray and dry pumice desert. Dry, that is, except for a trickle of a stream that eternally and jaggedly cut its way through the landscape, **evoking** the image of a broken heart.

At first we were able to walk on the stream's sides, but it soon became evident that the only way to keep going was to get our feet wet. From out of the blue, my friend stopped, and said, "Eddy, this has all of the trappings of an **ambush**. Keep an eye out."

Now, it was I who was becoming paranoid. All of the sudden the scenery had changed, and the walls became sheer vertical rises at a small waterfall. I had never seen anything like it; the pumice walls, eerily, created a hallway in the formation of what could best be described as a stairwell descending into hell. Looking at the topo map, it became clear that this path was leading perpendicularly into the side of a steep canyon, where we would surely encounter other streams flowing west.

From the bright sunshine above, we inched our way down into a four-foot vertical crevice, thereby plunging into near-total darkness. At about 60 yards into this stream-crafted anomaly, we reached a slightly round cathedral-like opening above us. It was roughly nine feet across. Without saying anything to each other, we stopped in unison to admire the formation. Without a word of forewarning, Tommy pulled his Luger and let fly with 14 shots. Looking up, my eyes locked with those of a large cougar, who was peering menacingly over the side 20 feet above us. I will never forget that sight or the thrilling spectacle, a split second later, of the beast's flying leap across the overhead expanse.

Before I could collect my wits, I was aware of pain shooting across my chest, and the first thing on my mind was that one of Tommy's shots had gone awry and found its way into me. Fortunately, it was only a red hot shell casing that had been ejected from the semi-automatic and burrowed itself into my flannel shirt.

As I shook it out, we both heaved a sigh of relief as we recovered from our abrupt back-to-back surprises. Knowing that the wild cat was in retreat, we were able to enjoy the rest of the afternoon. That was the only time that I found the old man's words of wisdom to be in error.

Moral of the story: Find good friends that you can trust—then trust their instincts.

26

Lightning Springs

Crater Lake in southern Oregon was once a massive mountain. That peak of long ago is now referred to as Mount Mazama. Before blowing its top, which transfigured it into Crater Lake, no one knows exactly how tall it was. Geologists now estimate it once stood somewhere between 11,000 and 12,000 feet.

The fact that the mighty Mazama was now a national park with top-notch camping areas and many well-kept trails was of particular interest to me. I could camp on the Pacific Crest Trail, take in the sights, and use most of the trails around the area for my cross-country altitude training. I particularly enjoyed the fact that during the summer I could go up every other week and spend less money for the summer than I would for a week at Steen's Mountain cross-country camp.

My favorite runs along the crater were Garfield Peak and Mount Scott. Both had elevations that started at about 7,000 feet and ended up at approximately 9,000 feet. Generally, I would run them in the early morning or the late evenings—or sometimes one in the morning and the other at night, to avoid being bothered by out-of-breath tourists.

The altitude was quite a change for me, as I spent most of my time at sea level. I often made my way up on a Friday night and stayed at Lightning Springs. It was a place that I knew well because I had camped there on numerous occasions. This particular trip was an exception; I arrived at noon after having spent the previous day in nearby Ashland taking in a **Shakespearean** theater production.

Finding myself with nothing better to do, and having a personal motto that sugar is **synonymous** with the life, I stopped in at Rim Village and ordered one of the restaurant's world-famous vanilla ice cream cones. The reason for the fame is the **exorbitant** price: two greenbacks. The cone's price tag isn't a **deterrent** when you see hundreds of other people eating them as if they were, in fact, on top of the world, by virtue of the experience. (I always brought along my spice pack and sprinkled on some **cardamom**, as if to say "mine is even better!") Well, at least it was a good conversation starter for anyone else indulging in that particular **decadence**.

Getting my 600-calorie fix out of the way would, of necessity, add an extra five-mile run on to my evening **agenda**. Soon after finishing my cone, I would don my 40-pound Lowe backpack and head down the trail to my No. 1 campsite. Somewhere beneath some mid-sized pine trees, in a flat area near the Pacific Crest Trail, I set up camp. It took mere minutes to accomplish that task, and fortunately, the only food I carried was tucked into plastic sacks in addition to their original foil and tin packs, and therefore of no interest to wildlife.

Throwing on my **Air Max Nikes**, the Pacific Crest Trail beckoned as I tied off an orange streamer and etched a couple of drag marks across the trail to indicate where to turn to get back up to my campsite. After going up any trail a few hundred yards, I had gotten into the habit of making a mental image of what the area would look like coming back, and I also tried to capture a mental **visualization** of particular features I might recognize in the dark, if my run took longer than expected.

Setting my running watch for 22 minutes, the evening jaunt I had planned seemed like a stroll in the park. At 22 minutes, the cry to turn around sounded, and the pleasant run back felt, blissfully, as if I were running downhill. On stopping to remove my marker, the short trip seemed almost a matter of **itinerary**. (I have discovered that if you take proper precautions in the woods most unexpected things don't occur.)

I cooked up my freeze-dried grub and an Army ration for dessert, then I took out my spice pack, which was encased doubly in plastic and then again in another plastic container so as not to take in moisture. Taking out my favorite spice, which is cayenne pepper, my **unpalatable** Army Meal Ready to Eat; (**MRE**) was foiled once again and transformed into a bearable, if not delectable meal.

Hoping for an early start in the morning, I was pleased that my **hollofil** camp pillow did its job well; I slept well. At about daybreak, a faint, low rumble **roused** me from my sleep. Thinking that the ruckus was the after-effect of a park ranger on a mission in some unfamiliar-sounding vehicle, my subconscious mind pressed me to wait a little longer before getting up.

A short while later, the rumbling intensified and the wheels in my mind started to burn rubber. What was that sound? No vehicles that I know of make that kind of sound, and besides this, the ground beneath me had begun to convulse--like an earthquake, I thought.

Concerned that the crater itself might be erupting, I jumped up and unzipped my tent, then stepped outside. Welcome to Kansas, I thought, as I looked around and took in the sight of a substantial herd of rogue cattle, at least 100 of them. Their combined weight, easily 100,000 pounds, trampling the ground around my tent was the reason for the mysterious earthquake.

About half were going around my tent on the left, and about half on the right. Most of the creatures didn't even look my way as they moved along their path, and I decided to walk to the other side to see why they weren't nudging or coming too close to my tent. When I had traveled 20 yards out from my tent in the direction the herd had come from, I turned around. Gazing into the low sunrise, I saw that my tent was blocking the sun's rays. The subsequent illusion occurred in such a manner that my tent appeared to be a large gray boulder, even though the structure was blue in color. Shaking my head, I fired up my Swiss-made Optimus camp stove and began making my morning coffee.

Moral of the story: Build your house on solid ground.

27

Marathon Man

During high school I was a proud member of an organization called the Vocational Industrial Clubs of America. Each year the local community college staged a Skills Day Competition, during which tuition scholarships were awarded to the winners in each industrial category of competition. These ranged from electronic theory to electrical house-wiring. For four years running I had won the electrical house-wiring event, and saved the full tuition scholarships until after graduation, when I presumably would move on to my next chapter of higher education.

The scholarships came in handy once I got to Southwestern Oregon Community College. In fact, I was able to comfortably live off my savings, but my love of pizza forced me to work a few hours a week part time at the nearby Godfathers Pizza. Relaxing in the student lounge a few days into my first term, I read on the notice board that the cross-country team only had four runners and was in desperate need of a fifth man. To officially qualify and score regulation points as a college team, a school was required to have a minimum of five people racing. Until I read that article, I hadn't even known that SWOCC had a cross-country team!

For the heck of it, I walked over to the gym and asked to speak to the cross-country coach, to ask if it was too late to swap my badminton class for cross-country. Mike, the jovial coach, looked at me expectantly, laughed, and said, "No, son, it's not too late—but you need to know that there's no credit given for a team sport."

Not wanting to diminish my interest, Mike asked me if I had run cross-country in high school. When I told him that I had, in fact, been the fifth man on my high school team during my senior year, he beamed broadly and said, "Eddy, you just made my day. Welcome aboard!"

There were many times when I regretted my commitment over the **ensuing** four weeks, which were punishingly challenging. I hadn't run competitions for almost a year and I was seriously out of shape physically. I also was carting around an extra 25 pounds than I had my senior year, and I was sometimes convinced that my legs were filled with lead!

Throughout the month-long training ordeal, I frequently developed Charley horse cramps, which at times were almost unbearable. By the time our competitive meets started, I was back down to an acceptable running weight, had gotten past the pre-season training pains and, for the most part, the Charley horses as well.

Fortunately for the team, we had four spectacular runners—who managed to take first through fourth place in nearly every race. Unfortunately, my personal performance was less **stellar**. I came in as the last-place scorer for every official college cross-country meet in which I competed. For two years I had been running a 5:35- to 5:45-per-mile pace, and just couldn't seem to go any faster, no matter how hard I tried.

But things were going better in other quarters. After two years at SWOCC I had accumulated the maximum number of transferable credits that a four-year institution would allow, and it was time to move on.

My decision to attend college in Ashland, Oregon, was a relatively easy one to make. The big draws were the campus' proximity to Crater Lake's hiking trails and Mount Ashland's inexpensive skiing. I also looked forward to taking in the town's famous theater offerings, available year-round but especially plentiful during Ashland's world-**renowned** Shakespearean Festival each summer.

A few days before registration, and a couple of days after finding an apartment, I walked into the athletic director's office only to find a **gatekeeper**. I asked the secretary if the cross-country coach was in, and she stared at me steely-eyed, with the gaze of a **tyrannical** oppressor. Do you have an appointment she seethed? Well; no, I began, I don't even know who he is yet. By chance he came out of his office just as we had begun talking.

He introduced himself as Monty and said "I'm on my way to a birthday party, can I help you out with something on the fly?" Walking out the door with him I asked if I might be able to run on the cross country team. He asked, "Have you run on any college teams before?" Yes, I replied, "I was fifth man for SWOCC for two years."

"Excellent," he replied, opening his car door. "Can you meet me at five o'clock tomorrow afternoon in my office?"

"Sure, see you then," I replied, and waved good-bye.

My next order of business was to press for an informal information interview with the unsuspecting manager of the local Pizza Shack. Walking in, I looked around and found the manager, who welcomed me with a courteous, "May I help you?" I told him that I was there to gather information on career opportunities and also to inquire about current job opportunities.

After informing me that there weren't any openings at the time, Tony eyed me quizzically, and said, "So, I'm curious about what brought you here, as I haven't advertised for any positions lately." I smiled and explained that I was a business major at the college and had worked in the pizza sector of fast food for six years--part time throughout high school and my first two years of college.

Sensing that my experience had piqued his interest, I handed him my **résumé** and four **letters of recommendation**. I added that I had also done some research on Pizza Shack, and knew that the company prefers to promote college graduates from within their system for managerial positions upon graduation.

Smiling now, Tony directed me to a table in the corner, and asked me to list the pizza places I had worked before. I replied, "Gino's, Pachinko's and Godfathers." I encouraged him to call my references, but also added, "Wouldn't you also like to know what I know about the pizza industry?"

"Well, go on and tell me, Eddy," he said. After about five minutes of relating the myriad money-saving ideas I had come up with while working at the other pizza places, Tony said, "OK, enough! How many hours per week would you need when a position opens up, Eddy?"

I told him that although I really didn't need a job just then, I would need a minimum of one hour a week to stay interested. "And since I live right over there in the apartments about 100 yards away, if an emergency were to arise, I suppose I could be on call if I was trained in all aspects of the restaurant's operation," I blurted out in a breathless **monologue**. "Oh, by the way, I have been known to be bribed by food in trade for work if the hour's part of your schedule isn't coming up within the **allotted tolerances**, if you know what I mean."

By this time, Tony was practically rolling on the floor, he was laughing so much. "Besides being amusing, Eddy, you're also the first person to care about my needs—and the first person who has made me feel like I really need you on my team. If you are sure about the one hour a week, I'll hire you."

I then offered to complete the paperwork that evening, and gently ventured, "And, Tony, if those two slightly stale single pizzas and a Coke are up for grabs, I can trade you for some dishes and some training off the clock tonight."

After 10 hours of hands-on training with Tony, everyone got the idea that he and I were longtime friends. They also figured that I was just going to be an on-call emergency fill-in, as I appeared to know how to do everything with little trouble and was talking with Tony about every thing from the cost of produce to health regulations, to industry food margins.

My first official on-the-clock hour of work was to be the next morning at 9 a.m. I was to meet Javier to learn Pizza Shack's precise and proper dough-**proofing** method. As luck would have it, the waitress who was supposed to come in at 9 a.m. didn't show. This was a minor inconvenience, but I was able to handle the task well enough. Just as I was finishing up, between grating carrots for the salad bar and studying how to properly cut up dough balls, the district manager walked in with Tony.

Puzzled as to why I was still there and then shaking his head about the missing-waitress ordeal, Tony introduced me as a potential future manager. The district manager (DM) asked me what I would do in the current situation if I was a manager.

This was where my business classes in school were about to pay off, I thought. In a quizzical reply, I asked, "Do all of your stores in the area staff two people in the restaurant at 9 in the morning?" "Yes, they do," the by now moderately **flummoxed** DM replied.

"Well, if I were you I would bring in someone like Javier at each Shack at 8 a.m. and have him do all of the restaurant prep work," I offered, adding that there is almost always extra time in-between for the dough proofing. When I saw that they were paying **rapt** attention, I continued: "Next, I wouldn't have any of the waitresses come in until 11. This would save an hour a day each day at all of your restaurants, simplify the work schedule and improve the morale of everyone involved. And if I'm right, you might stand to save between $40,000 and $50,000 a year."

By this time, both Tony and the DM were speechless. Pretending to be nonchalant, I concluded my short sermon by saying, "By the way, I hope you don't mind that I stayed two hours today instead of one. And if you'll excuse me, I have to clock out and, literally, go for a run!"

After my run, which is normally about seven miles, I showered and headed out to my 5 p.m. meeting. This time, when confronted with the **imperious** "do you have an appointment?" I was able to look the **obstinate** key-wielding dragon lady in the eye and say, **indubitably**, if not completely courteously, "Yes, ma'am, I do."

Just then a ripple of laughter issued from the back room, and a voice called out, "Come on back, Eddy!"

Minding my manners, I allowed the director, Monty to speak first. He told me that he had called Mike, my previous cross country coach. "Eddy, he told me that he was confident that you could run and finish a marathon for me," he said. I looked him in the eye, and said, "Well, I have run 36 miles straight before, but I'm really not into running marathons. All I really want to do is to run on the cross-country team."

He explained that he already had a very strong cross-country team. "But the problem, Eddy, is that none of the guys are willing to run a marathon for me during the track season." He told me about the dilemma at hand. The school was so close in the standings for the state championships in track and field, that all he really needed was someone to finish the Seaside Marathon. "That way, we'll get two points added before we even get to the state meet," he said. "Do you get the picture now?"

Sensing I was really not interested in resolving a onetime problem, he added, "If you really want to run cross-country, Eddy, we can let you run on the team. But there are only seven positions counted, and it's not likely at a 5:25 pace that you are ever going to place."

I assured Monty that I was used to that and explained that I didn't really have my heart set on placing. "I just enjoy cross-country, and I do well in all of the community sponsored running races in the off season," I replied.

"Oh, by the way, Eddy, I almost forgot the most important part," he said distractedly, as he pulled paperwork out of a drawer. "I have a one-year tuition scholarship that I've been saving for anyone who is willing to run the marathon."

I looked at Monty in utter disbelief, and asked, "Is it that important? At his nodding I said OK, I'll do it!" Handing me a pen, he said, "Sign here, Eddy, and you're officially on the cross-country team."

Moral of the story: Persistence pays off in the long run, and yes, we did win the state championship!

NOTES

NOTES

NOTES

NOTES

CPSIA information can be obtained
at www.ICGtesting.com
Printed in the USA
JSHW072056070223
37350JS00003B/3